I0601062

Breaking Arrow

Charon MC
Book 13

KHLOE WREN

Books by Khloe Wren

Charon MC:
Inking Eagle
Fighting Mac
Chasing Taz
Claiming Tiny
Chasing Scout
Tripping Nitro
Scout's Legacy
Mac's Destiny
Losing Bash
Finding Needles
Forging Blade
Taming Keys
Breaking Arrow

RBMC: SA:
Spark's rising
Croc's Pledge

Fire and Snow:
Guardian's Heart
Noble Guardian
Guardian's Shadow
Fierce Guardian
Necessary Alpha
Protective Instincts

Other Titles:
Fireworks
Scarred Perfection
Scandals: Zeck
FireStarter
Deception
Mine To Bear

ISBN: 978-0-6486896-9-0
Copyright © Khloe Wren 2021

Cover Credits:
Model: Joe Adams
Photographer: JW Photography
Digital Artist: Khloe Wren
Editing Credits:
Editor: Carolyn Depew of Write Right

This book is a work of fiction. The names, characters, places, and incidents are products of the writer's imagination or have been used fictitiously and are not to be construed as real. Any resemblance to persons, living or dead, actual events, locales or organizations is entirely coincidental.

All rights reserved. With the exception of quotes used in reviews, this book may not be reproduced or used in whole or in part by any means existing without written permission from the author.

If you are reading this book and did not purchase it, please delete and purchase it legally. Thank you for respecting the hard work of this author.

The author acknowledges the trademarked status and trademark owners of various products referenced in this work of fiction, which have been used without permission. The publication/use of these trademarks is not authorized, associated with, or sponsored by the trademark owners.

Acknowledgements

As with every book I write, I couldn't do it without the unending support of my husband and daughters. Especially when I struggle like I have this year with my mental health, my family and their support are priceless.

To my editing team, Carolyn, Rainy and Jen, thank you so much for pulling out all the stops to help me make this deadline.

So many people helped with various research for this story, I'm sure I don't have everyone's names in my notes and for that I apologize. Stacey, thank you for all the Houston knowledge help and everything else. Janelle & Lauren for your hairdressing expertise! Lexy and the other awesome people in the Trauma Fiction FB group for your advice on various injuries.

My awesome street team, thank you for the support and help: Fran Reading named Dr. Lilith Mason. I mixed up suggestions from Melissa Cooke Hawley & Eden Bradley to come up with Lone Oak Rehab Center, and Tracie Runge for Pieces to Peace, the Charon MC's new rehab center they'll build soon.

To Janine and Fiona, so many fictional trees were grown to get this book written. I couldn't have done it without you both.

Lastly, to you who's reading this. Thank you so much for taking a chance with me and I hope you enjoy reading Breaking Arrow as much as I did writing it.

xo

Khloe Wren

Biography

Khloe Wren lives in rural South Australia with her husband, two daughters and an ever changing list of animals!

She started writing in 2013 and has published over 30 books since then in the romantic suspense genre. She writes both paranormal and contemporary stories, including her best selling series Charon MC.

Khloe enjoys writing outside of the box and she loves her heroes strong, and her heroines even stronger.

Charon:

Char·on \ˈsher-ən, ˈker-ən, -än\

In Greek mythology, the Charon is the ferryman who takes the dead across either the river Styx or Acheron, depending on whether the soul's destination is the Elysian Fields or Hades.

Chapter 1

Friday 14th July 2006
DeRidder, Louisiana
Tabitha

Hiding from the drug dealer in our living room wasn't how I'd intended to end my day, but it sadly wasn't all that unexpected. My stepfather, Mikey, had a drug problem. I'd been ignoring it over the past three years because I had no fucking clue what to do about it. I'd stupidly hoped that at some point, Mikey would snap out of his grief and quit. Return to his former self or something.

A childlike dream that, at nineteen, I should have known better than to even entertain for a moment.

Since I wanted to avoid Volt, the asshole Mikey bought his drugs from, at all costs, I was stuck in my bedroom with nothing to do but stare at my little brother Todd's empty bed, and hope that tonight Volt would leave without any of the drama he'd brought with him last week.

It'd been a week since that fucker out there had come around with his enforcers to collect Mikey's overdue payment. Naturally, he didn't have the damn money, so the enforcers had beaten the shit out of him. He still sported the bruises, but that wasn't the worst thing they'd done. With perfect timing, I'd come home from work just in time to see one of the big brutes snap Todd's arm.

My little brother was seven fucking years old and completely innocent in this whole thing.

With him screaming in pain, I'd raced to my bedroom and retrieved the battered old tin from the back of my closet. With tears blurring my vision, I emptied out all the tips from work I'd been stashing away, trying to save enough to get me and Todd out of this piece of shit trailer. After I handed over all the money I had, the man who'd hurt Todd had given me a wink and nod before he'd followed Volt and the others out, like he hadn't just broken a child's arm.

I'd gathered up Todd and with the help of a neighbor who owned a car, took him to the hospital. The staff there had called in child services and now my brother was in foster care.

I swiped the tears from my eyes and blew out a breath. I missed Todd so much. For the past three years, I'd been more of a mother than a sister to him. Ever since our mother had passed away after giving birth to our stillborn sister. That had been the beginning of the end of life as we'd known it.

Well, for me that had happened when my own father had died in a workplace accident. He'd been crushed between two beams on a construction site when I'd been just four years old. Momma had struggled after that to earn enough money to keep a roof over our heads until we'd moved here to the trailer park.

Eleven years later, she started seeing a drifter who'd come to the park. The moment Momma told him she was pregnant with Todd, he'd vanished, never to be seen again. It had been three years after that when Momma found Mikey. He'd been a long-haul truck driver and had loved all three of us. Early on he'd been a great father and husband, whenever he was in town. Then Momma got pregnant again.

I swiped angrily at the tears that continued to flow. I hated crying. It didn't fix a damn thing. Didn't bring back my family. Didn't stop Mikey from turning to cocaine to deal with his grief. Didn't stop him from spending every dime we had on getting his next fix.

Frustration built and sick of staring at where Todd should have been sitting here with me, I rose to crack open the door, hoping to hear if Volt and Mikey were nearly done.

Volt's voice was all smooth charm. "You know, we can make a deal if you don't have the money. You don't have to leave it until after I'm forced to involve my enforcers. That girl of yours is pretty enough to pull in some bank. Let me have her and we'll work something out."

Mikey stood from his seat, fists clenched down by his sides. "No, you can't. You don't understand, she's all I have left!"

Volt had his arms crossed over his chest as he continued to stare down Mikey.

"Her or the drugs, Mikey. You can't have both in your life. Not anymore."

I closed the door, as quietly as possible. Volt's words rung in my ears as on shaky legs I stumbled toward my bed. He wanted to own me. I'd previously turned him down, more than once, when he'd asked me out on a date. My rejections hadn't stopped him from ogling me every chance he got. The man was a creep who'd made my skin crawl from the very first time I met him. But I'd never in a million years thought he'd want to buy me like I was a pet.

Ignoring the tears that now ran unchecked down my cheeks, I took a deep breath and forced down my scattered thoughts. I needed to escape before Mikey gave me up. I knew he would. Eventually, the need for cocaine would overtake his need to keep me around. The fact I looked just like my mother would only get me so far.

Going over to my closet, I pulled out my duffle bag. The first thing I grabbed was my most prized possession: a framed photo of me, Todd, and Momma that Mikey had taken about a year before her death. Then, I shoved in as much clothing as I could grab before I rushed over to the window which, thankfully, slid silently open to allow me a quick exit.

Memories of how Mikey had been before he'd become an addict flashed through my mind as I crept down the side of our place. Volt never went anywhere alone, so even though he was the only one inside with Mikey, I knew he'd have two or more of his meathead goons out here watching. Pushing away thoughts of better days, I focused on getting through the trailer park unnoticed. By the time I hit the highway out of DeRidder, I was back to thinking about the past and allowed myself a few moments to grieve for that Mikey, the man who'd been a doting father to me and Todd before I stuck my thumb out to hitch a ride away from everything I'd ever known.

I knew hitchhiking was dangerous, especially for a young woman alone, but I had to take the risk. It was the only way to be sure I could get far enough out of town before Mikey or Volt realized I'd heard them and left for good. And really, compared to what Volt had planned for me, what worse trouble could I end up in with a stranger?

The answer to that question had all sorts of horrors flicking through my mind until a car with a nice-looking older woman driving, pulled up to offer me a ride. She lowered the passenger window before speaking.

"Where you heading, sugar?"

I gave her a smile as I shrugged. "So long as it's a long way from here, I don't care where I land."

"I'm heading to Barker, Texas. It's up in the panhandle and about a nine-hour drive from here. That far enough for you?"

I grinned, thankful to whatever higher power had put this woman in my path.

"That sounds perfect."

"Well, climb on in and let's get moving. I'm Kerri. What's your name, honey?"

I slipped my bag off my shoulder and hopped into the nice comfortable car, dropping my bag between my feet as I reached for the seatbelt. I'd never been inside such a fancy car. It had to be pretty new.

"I'm Tabitha. This is a really nice car."

"Well, since work makes me drive across two states on a regular basis, the least they can do is give me a nice car to do it in," she said.

I nodded as I continued to stare in awe at all the modern stuff on the dash. I had no clue what most of it was. It looked a lot different to the old Chevy Mikey drove around before he sold it to buy his drugs.

"So, Tabitha, we have a long drive ahead of us and I need you to help me stay awake. How about you tell me what has you running so far from home?"

I turned to stare into her face, trying to gauge what she'd do with the information.

"In a nutshell, my stepfather's an addict and his dealer told him he could pay his debt by handing me over to him. I overheard them and got the hell out of there before they could act on it."

Her eyes widened as her mouth dropped open.

"Where's your momma at?" she asked.

Tears pricked my eyes as I settled back and started telling Kerri all about the tragic series of events that had led to this moment where I was running for my life, trusting a stranger to keep me safe.

Kerri seemed to want to know every little detail, often asking questions for more information on most everything I told her. By the time the sun began to rise, I was sure she knew as much about me as I did.

"What's your plan once we reach Barker?" she asked.

I shrugged as I looked out the window at the scenery zooming by.

"I honestly don't know. My plan ended with escaping DeRidder." I turned to face her. "Why? Do you have a suggestion?"

Part of me was hoping she'd offer to take me home with her. She was already someone I respected; she was straight down the line, didn't bullshit.

"Well, honey, I wish I could simply take you home with me, but my place is tiny, and I travel so much, I'd rarely be there for you but there's this new church in town, The Chosen Way. Pastor Godfrey, who runs it, put an ad in the local paper last week for a housekeeper. I could give him a call for you, if you think that's something you'd like to do? It'd give you a safe place to live, and a way to make some money you can save up while you decide what you want to do next."

I chewed on my lower lip as I thought over the offer. If the man was a pastor, that should be safe enough, right? And it's not like I had any other options to choose from.

"I can keep a house clean no trouble, and cook meals for him if he wants that. If you could make the call for me, that'd be great."

Kerri nodded as she put on her turn signal and changed lanes. "Excellent, next time we stop for gas I'll give him a call."

It would beat living on the streets, and hopefully could be a steppingstone onto something better.

Tabitha

I was more than ready to end the drive when we finally made it to Barker, Texas. Nine hours was way too long to spend sitting a car, I didn't care how comfortable it was. Kerri pulled up in front of a large house on a street that looked like it was straight out of a sitcom on T.V. Every lawn was perfectly manicured, every drive was paved and clean. Completely opposite to the trailer park in DeRidder.

Shutting off the engine, she turned to face me. "Here we are. Pastor Godfrey said he'd be home. But I'll still walk up with you, make sure he's there."

I gave her a smile as I murmured a thanks, then grabbed my bag and climbed out of her vehicle. Nerves had me hesitating on the sidewalk. What was I doing? This was crazy! I'd just travelled over nine hours with a perfect stranger, and I was about to go see another stranger about living in his house and working for him.

With a concerned frown, Kerri rested a palm on my forearm. "Tabitha? You okay? You don't have to do this. I just thought it might be a good place for you to find your feet, but there's certainly no pressure on you to say yes."

Closing my eyes, I blew out a breath before straightening my shoulders and looking back to Kerri. She was a lovely woman who was offering me a hand up. I needed to be more grateful and stop making her feel like she'd done me a disservice.

"No, I want to give this a try. I've got nothing else, so really it's this or finding a vacant park bench somewhere."

She gave me a sad smile as I moved past her and up the path to knock on the front door. As I stood there, questioning my sanity for what I was doing, I wondered if I shouldn't turn and run down the street. A click preceded the door swinging open before I could act on my swirling thoughts.

My breath caught in my throat when the crystal blue gaze of the man who'd answered the door caught mine. They were mesmerizing and if this was the pastor Kerri had told me about, I could see how he could be good at his job. His neatly trimmed beard and short dark brown hair together with his eyes made him look friendly and approachable.

His gaze moved from me over to Kerri, who'd come to stand beside me, and he smiled.

"Kerri, I'm so glad you've made it safely home once again, and this must be the young woman you called me about earlier. Tabitha, it is a pleasure to meet you. My name is Pastor Roger Godfrey, why don't you come in and we can chat over a coffee? Kerri, will you be joining us?"

"I wish I could, but I have to get going." She turned to me and pulled me in for a hug. "Take care of yourself, Tabitha, and I'll see you around."

She turned and left as Roger shifted to the side and indicated I should enter his home. Taking a deep breath, I stepped over the threshold and into the house, sealing my decision.

"The kitchen is this way."

It was a surprise to see a few other men moving around the house as I followed him through to the kitchen. After glancing into a few rooms, I frowned. The decor didn't add up to what I'd imagined a man of Roger's age would have. He seemed to be in his early to mid-thirties, while the house was decorated in a manner I imagined an older woman would use. All the frills, lace and floral prints didn't seem masculine at all. Not that I'd seen many homes outside of trailer parks, so maybe I had it wrong. Or maybe Pastor Godfrey was married and his wife liked all this stuff.

Entering the kitchen, he indicated the table. "Take a seat while I make our coffees. How do you take yours?"

"Black, no sugar, thanks."

I slid into a high back chair and looked around the room, my gaze catching on the display cabinet mounted on the wall that was filled with souvenir teaspoons. I was still staring at the collection when Roger set a mug in front of me.

"Agnus had some strange addictions. This was her house. She very generously donated it along with her possessions to The Chosen Way. We haven't had time to sort through everything yet."

I nodded and reached for my coffee to take a drink. It was hot and strong, just how I liked it, and I enjoyed the taste as I tried to work out how to respond. I had no clue what to say. Why on earth would someone donate everything they owned to a church? But I didn't want to come across as rude, so I lifted my cup and sipped while pretending like it was all totally normal.

"Kerri didn't tell me much about you. What brought you here to Barker?"

Carefully setting the cup down on the coaster, I licked my lips as I decided how much to tell this man.

"My mother passed away a few years ago. I was living with my stepfather, but something happened that made it impossible for me to stay there, so I left. I was lucky that Kerri stopped to give me a ride. She was on her way home and offered to bring me all the way with her. I think she wanted some company for the long drive." I looked down as I took another mouthful of the hot coffee before continuing. "So, here I am."

"And where did you start your travels?"

"I was born and raised across the border in Louisiana."

He smiled and sat a little straighter. "It's been years since I've been to Louisiana. I've always enjoyed walking around the French Quarter."

I smiled sadly. "I've never been. Before yesterday, I'd never left DeRidder, never had the opportunity to."

His eyes widened. "You'd never left your hometown? Not even for school trips?"

Forcing down a wave of sadness, I took another drink to give myself a moment.

"There was never the money for me to do school excursions or anything else." I shrugged. "It wasn't a big deal."

He was frowning when I risked a glance at his silence.

"Do you think your stepfather will worry for you? Maybe come looking?"

I bit my lip and thought about it. "I don't think so, and even if he did, he'd never be able to afford to travel this far from home."

There was also no way he'd be able to trace that it was Kerri who'd picked me up, let alone where we were heading, but he could work that out without me telling him.

"Would you mind giving me his name and what he looks like? Just in case he ever does show up."

I didn't want to believe he could find me. The Mikey who raised me was long gone; the addict now in his place was no one I wanted to be around.

"He seriously has no way of tracking me here. I can't imagine him leaving Louisiana for any reason, let alone to look for me. He lost himself after my mother passed. I think something deep inside him died along with her and he's an empty shell now."

"At least give me his name. Just in case."

"Mikey Trahan."

He reached over and gave my forearm a light squeeze. "Thank you for trusting me with that. It was such a blessing Kerri was the one who stopped for you, got you safely away. She told you I'm looking for a housekeeper, yes?"

Happy to be moving on to a different topic, I nodded and then continued to sip at my coffee.

"Have you done this kind of work before?"

I finished my drink and set the empty cup back onto the table.

"Ever since my momma passed, I've taken care of where we lived. It was nothing as grand as this, but I know how to keep a house clean. I worked in a diner and can cook for you if you need that, too."

He smiled at me and his blue eyes sparkled in a way that held me mesmerized for a few moments before I blinked and broke the spell. A shiver ran down my spine as an image of a snake popped into my mind for some reason.

"That sounds perfect. And perhaps you could help us sort through Agnus' various collections so we can get them valued."

"I can do that."

Cleaning and cooking were nothing but jobs to me, but going through an elderly woman's treasures would be fun. I couldn't wait to see what interesting things I'd find. As he started to explain how much he could pay me, on top of the fact I could live here free of charge, I started getting excited about this fresh start. Seemed like overhearing that conversation between Volt and Mikey had been a blessing in disguise.

A shiver ran down my spine as a kernel of doubt crept in. I really hoped this wasn't a *too good to be true* thing and that Pastor Godfrey and his men were exactly who they seemed to be on the surface; good, honest men who only wanted to help others.

Chapter 2

Godfrey

After showing Tabitha to her room, I made my way back to my office. She'd been on the road all night and from the way she was struggling to contain her yawns, I gathered she hadn't slept much, so I'd instructed her to take today to settle in, to have a nap and relax. Once I was safely behind my desk, I booted up my computer and logged into the camera feeds. As soon as I'd hung up from Kerri, I'd rushed to get them installed in the room I planned to give to Tabitha so I'd be able to watch my newest acquisition whenever I wanted to.

As the feed came up, I relaxed back into my chair and watched as she carefully put her few belongings away in the dresser. She was a beautiful girl. Long chocolate brown hair with just a hint of a wave to it, stunning hazel eyes, and flawless skin. She'd fetch a good price and I could guess that was what her stepfather was attempting to do. Oh well, his loss was my gain. Although I didn't plan to sell her off just yet. A sweet young innocent girl like Tabitha had more than one use.

A knock on my door had me hovering my hand over the keyboard to exit from the feed until I saw it was my right-hand man, Phil.

"Morning, boss."

He shifted around to stand beside me to watch as Tabitha moved from the bedroom to the bathroom across the hall with a change of clothes. With a flick of a switch, we watched her take in the bathroom that still looked like an elderly woman had decorated it. I couldn't wait to strip all that old biddy's shit out of this place, but it had to be done carefully so others in town didn't see through my ruse.

Being a conman wasn't as easy as most people thought. It took a lot of careful planning, and a whole lot of acting.

"What's the plan with this one? We training her? Because, let me tell you, I'll be happy to help out with that."

I shook my head as we watched her strip, revealing more flawless skin and subtle curves.

"Not yet. I want to use her to build goodwill in the town first. It's a good look to take in a sweet innocent runaway and give her a job and roof over her head. When we have to move on, we'll reevaluate."

"Fuck, look at those tits."

I gave Phil a nod. She was, without a doubt, a gorgeous young woman.

"No touching her, not yet. If she turns out to be a good housekeeper and does well spreading the word around town, she might just prove more useful to us by bringing in others. There is also the matter of Kerri if we decide to start training her while we're still in Barker. There's no benefit in getting rid of her other than freeing up Tabitha at this stage. If we can use Tabitha to bring her into the church and tithe her possessions to us, then we can ensure she has an accident."

Phil let out a sigh. "I hear you. No touching. But fuck, if you change your mind, you let me know because I want in on that."

The steam from the shower began to fog up the lens and I turned from the screen to Phil.

"I need you to investigate her stepfather. Find out if he's looking for her at all. We don't want trouble following her to our doorstep. His name is Mikey Trahan and he lives in DeRidder, Louisiana. I need you to deal with him and anyone he may have contacted to help him track down his stepdaughter."

That perked up Phil's mood and with a broad grin, he gave me a nod. "Consider it done."

I bit back my chuckle as he strode out of my office. I knew he'd do as I requested. Phil lived for these little errands. Mr. Trahan, along with anyone he'd gotten to assist him in finding Tabitha, would be having a deadly accident in the near future.

I shifted my attention back to Tabitha, watching her blurred form move around as she finished her shower. I needed to upgrade that camera, maybe put in a few more because I rather liked watching her.

Wednesday 7th July 2010
Cooper, Texas
Tabitha

Time flew by as Pastor Godfrey kept me busy with all he needed me to do. Before I knew it, days had turned to weeks, to months then years. I loved being a part of The Chosen Way, supporting Pastor Godfrey and his men in any way I could as they helped people in each place as much as they could before we moved on to help another town. Mostly it was doing what I'd started out doing. I kept the house where he lived clean and tidy, cooked his meals, washed his clothes… and other housework-type stuff, but I also helped him sort through donations so they could be sold off. Like I had with all of Agnus' things back in Barker. Pastor Godfrey had someone else look after the actual selling of everything, but it was my job to sort, clean, pack, and write descriptions.

From the beginning, I always made sure when I did the weekly grocery shopping, I dropped into the post office to send a letter to Todd and to see if he'd written one back to me. Every new town we came to, I'd go into the post office and sort out an arrangement that I could get mail sent directly to them rather than wherever we were living. I'd never told Pastor Godfrey — or anyone else — about my brother. I wasn't sure why exactly, but something deep inside had me holding my tongue on that little bit of information.

I treasured the few letters Todd managed to write to me. He didn't write as often as I did, but I didn't mind. I cherished each word he wrote about how his life was in his foster home, how good it was for him there. How he now could go on school excursions and play weekend sports.

In one of the first letters he'd sent me, he told me about Mikey's death. He'd fallen asleep with a lit cigarette in his hand and it had burned down the trailer. The news had torn my heart open. That Mikey had fallen so far from that man he'd once been to die in such a way.

Todd was my only contact outside of The Chosen Way. Kerri had been good to me early on, but by the second move, we lost contact. I missed chatting with her but between her travel schedule and my shifting around, it got too hard and we both just sort of let it slide. The fact Pastor Godfrey liked having me on call twenty-four/seven didn't help with me making any new friends in each town we relocated to. Even at the services The Chosen Way ran, Pastor Godfrey would keep me too busy to stop and chat for long.

I didn't mind. He paid me well, and on top of my wage, he provided me with my uniform — black slacks and fitted white button-up shirts — all my food plus accommodation, of course. That meant I didn't have much else to spend money on, so it just went into my savings account and grew, waiting for me to choose what my next step in life would be.

I still wasn't entirely sure what that would be. I was

good at being a housekeeper but that didn't seem like a high enough goal. I mean surely, I should want more, right? Most kids dreamed of doing something big when they were little, didn't they?

I remembered kids at school always talking about wanting to be a firefighter, cop, nurse, lawyer, or doctor. But I'd always had simpler dreams. Earning enough to live in a nice clean house and have enough food in the fridge had been my goals.

I had those things now so I could dream bigger, but I had no idea what. And I had no one to talk to about it. It was hard to have a conversation via letter with Todd. He'd been asking me to get a computer so we could email each other but Pastor Godfrey did not like technology and didn't want me having such things. He had a computer and mobile, of course, but he had to in order to keep The Chosen Way running. I didn't need either to do my work.

With a sigh, I wiped down the kitchen table and returned the cloth to the sink. We were prepping to move again. Pastor Godfrey had been commuting between here and the new town for the past month, getting things ready for us to all head over there, and I'd been packing up each room into boxes for the move. I wasn't sure where we were going. He didn't tell me anymore. After the second move, he'd told me I didn't need to worry about such things. He'd make sure I was taken care of and that was all that mattered. And he was right; he had always taken care of me, and it really didn't matter, so I'd stopped asking and just went with the flow.

After collecting a couple of folded boxes from the garage and the packing tape from the kitchen, I headed to the rear bedroom to start getting that room sorted out for moving. It was the room Ronald, one of Godfrey's most trusted men, had been using but he'd told me last night that he didn't have time to pack it up and asked me to do it today after lunch. It was one of the last rooms to be boxed up so I knew Pastor Godfrey would want me to get it done quickly.

Lost in my thoughts of everything I needed to do before the move, I didn't realize the room wasn't empty until it was too late.

Chapter 3

Tabitha

I'd quickly learned that Pastor Godfrey preferred a quiet home, so I was careful to open the door silently. The moment the door seal was broken, noises filtered out that had me frozen to the spot. Within the room there were three men, including Ronald, and a young woman, a teen, between them. All were naked. The woman had welts and marks all over her. Tears tracked mascara down her face as the men shoved their dicks into her, one in her vagina, one that had to be inside her ass, and Ronald, who stood near her head, held one hand fisted in her hair and the other around his erection, guiding it to her closed mouth.

"Open the fuck up, slut. It's your new life. Pretty little thing like you will bring in serious bank once we get you all trained up. Quit your crying and swallow my cock down. Need to get you nice and good at deep-throating a big fat cock for your new life. And don't even think about fucking biting me. You do, and we'll string you up and beat the hell outta you again before I fuck your throat."

I'd never heard such language in my life; could barely believe what I was seeing and hearing. These were Pastor Godfrey's most trusted men, who worked in the church, who were kind and gentle.

I stood frozen until Ronald looked up and caught me watching. He smirked and winked before he spoke to me.

"Hey babe, been waiting on you. Wanna come join in?"

With a squeak, I dropped the boxes and tape and ran toward Pastor Godfrey's office. Surely he didn't realize what his men were doing? I was about to slam through his door when I remembered his need for quiet and slowed down to a more sedate pace. Normally, I'd knock and wait for him to come and open the door but I didn't want the other men to catch me before I could speak to him.

I winced when I saw Phil was with him discussing something. I didn't want an audience to tell Pastor Godfrey what I'd witnessed. They were so engrossed in their conversation, they hadn't noticed I'd come in yet. I silently closed the door and leaned against it for a moment, trying to calm my heart rate before I spoke up and announced my presence.

"So, it's all set? Her death was ruled an accident and the estate is in the bank?"

"You know better than to doubt me, boss. Of course, it was ruled an accident. I'm good at what I do."

For the second time in the last few minutes, I found myself stunned speechless. Was nothing as it appeared?

Godfrey frowned as he looked over at me. "Tabitha? What are you doing rushing in here unannounced like this?"

I shook my head and turned to open the door, intending on running straight out the front door and away from these madmen. A large hand smacked against the door, banging it shut and pushing me up against the wood. My breath slammed out of my lungs and before I could think to fight, Phil had both my wrists in one of his against the door over my head. His other hand wrapped in my hair, much like Ronald had done to that other girl. He pulled my head back and to the side so he could have access to my neck. A shudder ran through me and tears pricked my eyes as Phil ground his hard erection against my ass while he licked up my neck.

"Been waiting four years to get a taste of you, girl. Fuck." He groaned the last word.

"Use this to bind her hands behind her back."

Godfrey's voice wasn't the smooth, calm tone he normally used with me but a harsh bark I'd never heard from him before. I tried to wriggle free, but Phil was so much stronger than me I didn't stand a chance against him. Within seconds, I had a zip tie around my wrists and was shoved, back first, against the wall beside the door.

Godfrey stood before me, arms crossed over his chest. Chills raced over my skin when he ran his gaze up and down my body as though he knew what lay beneath my clothes. "You didn't answer my question, Tabitha. What caused you to enter my office in such a manner?"

I flicked my gaze between the two men. I could see Phil knew what had happened, but I couldn't tell if Pastor Godfrey already knew.

"I went to pack up Ronald's room as he asked me to and he was in there, with a couple of others. And a girl. Doing things I didn't think you knew about..." I let my voice trail off, because the glint in his eyes removed all doubt.

He knew exactly what I'd walked in on.

"Hmm, seems as though Ronald got impatient waiting for my permission and set you up to fall, my little Martha."

I frowned. Martha? Who the hell was Pastor Godfrey on about now? Had he lost his mind or something? That would explain this craziness. As pieces clicked into place in my mind, I realized Godfrey hadn't suddenly lost his mind. He was an evil conman who preyed on the elderly and lonely.

He went back to his desk and opened a drawer. I tried to see what he was doing but Phil had wrapped a fist in my hair again and I couldn't turn my head that far. He shifted so he had a leg between mine, pressing up against my sex as he ground his erection in against my hip. A whimper escaped my throat when his free hand went to my shirt, flipping open the buttons. Pastor Godfrey returned to stand in front of me, his gaze on the flesh Phil was revealing. "Such pretty flawless skin."

I shuddered as bile rose up my throat. Visions of that other girl, Nina, flashed in my mind. My future would now hold similar treatment, I was sure.

I frowned at the chunky-looking black metal collar-type necklace Pastor Godfrey raised into my field of vision. "Move her out from the wall so I can get this on her."

Removing his knee from between my thighs, Phil stepped back and using his fist in my hair shifted me so Pastor Godfrey could come up behind me and wrap the necklace he'd retrieved around my neck. I wasn't sure what type of catch the thing had but it took him a few minutes to get it sorted, giving Phil time to finish undoing my shirt and move onto tugging at my bra with his free hand.

"When you're done, undo her fucking bra. Damn thing is in my way."

"Cut it all off. Her uniform is going to be changing anyway. No more pants or underwear for our little toy. We'll need easy access whenever we want it."

Pastor Godfrey finished what he was doing and returned to stand in front of me while Phil took a knife from his belt to my bra, slicing up the center so my breasts spilled free. I winced when Pastor Godfrey palmed my breasts before tugging and twisting my nipples while Phil tightened his grip in my hair until tears pricked my eyes.

"Thanks to what you've seen today, things will be changing for you. You are no longer Tabitha. You are my very own Martha. You will run around busying yourself doing anything I ask." He smirked at me. "That includes bending over so I can fuck you, or getting on your knees to suck my cock. Or any of my men. You are to do anything you're asked. Your new accessory is not just for decoration. It's a shock collar. You disobey, you'll get a shock. We'll be moving you to the new house today and once there, we'll set the collar so you'll get a shock if you leave the house. You are to be seen but not heard. If you're good, you'll stay as my silent housekeeper and fuck toy. If you misbehave, you'll be trained just like little Nina down the hall and put up for sale. Do you understand?"

I couldn't hold back the tears as I nodded. What choice did I have? Those mesmerizing steel blue eyes that had once soothed me were now all the snake I'd glimpsed that first day. Pastor Godfrey was a monster. He'd lured me in and now he'd well and truly caught me in his trap.

My heart rate was thumping so hard I could hear it in my ears by the time Phil released my hair and began cutting away the rest of my clothes. Closing my eyes, I prayed for death, prayed my heart would beat so fast it would burst and kill me, because I feared that was the only way I was ever going to escape this new hell I'd found myself in. Guess escaping Volt and landing with Godfrey wasn't the blessing I had first thought it was.

May 2017
Riverton, Texas
Martha/Tabitha

In complete silence I slipped through the shadows of the house back to my room. In the last six years, I'd gotten pretty damn good at making myself invisible. I'd discovered early on that out of sight was truly out of mind. Especially after that first year and the novelty of me had worn off.

Turned out Pastor Godfrey along with his men had all been eyeing me the entire time I'd worked for him and when the forbidden fruit had become available, they'd all been excited to get their turn. I prayed daily that first month for death, before I realized God either wasn't listening or didn't care. I struggled to believe in a higher power that would allow people like Godfrey and his men to roam the earth.

Now I did everything I could to not feel at all, to not think. I was little more than a robot. I cleaned, cooked, and hid. The rapes and other abuse had lessened over the years, but they hadn't stopped. Phil in particular still liked to grab me at least a few times a week. Sometimes daily. Sadly, I could tell whenever they'd gotten a new girl to train for the auction block who took his fancy, because he'd leave me alone for several days.

It broke my heart how many people Godfrey must have sold into sexual slavery over the years. I was sure I'd only known about a fraction of the ones he'd caught since I'd become Martha, and he'd been running The Chosen Way for years before I came to him. So many lives he'd destroyed but there was nothing I could do to save any of them.

Hell, I couldn't even save myself. I'd fought back a few times early on when the men had gotten rough and each time Godfrey had pulled out his evil little remote and shocked me. Having electricity shoot through your neck and down your spine was not an experience I'd wish on anyone. Well, except for assholes like Godfrey and his men. I'd happily pull the trigger on them to be electrocuted.

Once inside my room, I closed the door and leaned back against it with a sigh of relief. I'd made it. Generally speaking, no one bothered me in my room these days. I wasn't sure why but was grateful for it. They had early on, and I still struggled to sleep fearing how I'd be woken up, but as the novelty had worn off, I guess they weren't so desperate to fuck me that they could be bothered going out of their way to seek me out.

In reality, it was probably because it was at night when they normally trained the other victims. That day I'd walked in on them was a set up. Ronald had told me straight he and Phil got sick of waiting and set me up to find out what they did, so they could have at me.

I'd taken a couple steps away from the door when a hand slipping over my mouth had me freezing, holding my breath. Before I could open my eyes to see who'd been waiting in my dark room, warm breath washed over my ear.

"Shh, Tabitha. It's just me. Todd."

This had to be a dream, but I didn't remember falling asleep. I hadn't been called Tabitha in six years; the name sounded foreign to my ears. Struggling to believe this was real, I pulled away from him and spun to look at who had found out about Todd and would be so cruel as to pretend to be my long-lost brother. No one should know about him. The more I found out about Godfrey and his evil nature, the more thankful I was that I'd kept Todd's existence a secret.

Once Godfrey had locked the collar on my throat, no one bothered to even attempt to hide what really went on. I'd felt like such a fool that I hadn't picked up on any of it. The first time Phil had come to me on his own, he'd taken great pleasure in telling me that it had been him who had gone and killed Mikey, setting it up to look like an accident. That he was an expert at it and anyone I tried to reach out to would suffer the same fate. I asked him if he'd already killed Kerri and he'd shaken his head but told me he would if I tried to draw her back into my life.

I rapidly learned that killing people in "accidents" was part of what Godfrey and his crew did. They normally focused on older single men and women who had no family left, but that didn't stop them from pulling in someone younger if they could. Anyone they came across was fair game. They'd use the guise of being a church and how much they helped people to get them to agree to "tithe" their estates to them. Not only did they focus on getting them to change their Wills, but they would also somehow manage to get people to transfer land and assets to them while they were still living.

I'd like to say it was all so outrageous that surely no one would fall for it, but I did. Well, I had no assets to give but I was responsible for bringing in a number of their victims in those early years. I'd had no idea what they'd been doing but that didn't lessen my guilt over feeling responsible. Godfrey had taken full advantage of having taken in a "poor runaway". I hated that I'd fallen for his bullshit so easily.

The other thing Godfrey and his crew were involved in was human trafficking. It was only because, when Kerri brought me to him, Godfrey needed a housekeeper and someone to help build his reputation around town that prevented me from being sold off on the auction block like so many others. Along with the shock collar, that was what Godfrey still threatened me with if I did something he didn't like, but I didn't fear it anymore. I was already living that life and it no longer mattered to me who held my leash.

Shaking free the thoughts, I focused back on the now, frowning at the man in my room.

"Don't lie to me. Who are you?"

He stepped toward me, holding up his palm in a gesture of peace. "It's really me, Tabitha. I'd turn on the light to show you, but I think there might be a camera in here. It's taken me days to work out where the outside ones are so I could get past them. I came to get you free. Fuck, Tabitha, I've been looking for you for over a year. I can't believe I've finally found you."

Chapter 4

Martha/Tabitha

My eyes had adjusted to the dark now and I could make out enough of Todd's features to believe this was indeed an older version of the boy I'd left behind all those years ago. I crept toward him and as soon as I was close enough, he reached for me, pulling me in so he could hug me close.

"Fuck, sis." He pressed a kiss to my temple and inhaled a shaky breath as I relaxed against his warm body.

My eyes pricked with tears; it felt that good to be able to hug him after so many years.

"Why'd you come?" I whispered.

He huffed out a breath. "Why? You're my sister, I love you, and you stopped writing. Of course, I'm going to come looking! When—with no warning—the letters stopped, I knew something must have gone wrong. My foster parents didn't believe me and refused to help me search for you, so I had to wait until I was old enough to be able to do it on my own. By the time I turned sixteen, I couldn't wait any longer, so I left on my birthday and haven't been back there since. I've been all over Texas following that fucker's trail looking for you. He changed his church's name for a while and that threw me off his trail for a bit, but when he went back to using The Chosen Way here in Riverton, I caught up with him. We really need to get moving, though. We'll talk more later. I don't want us to get caught."

I couldn't love my brother more, but I was going to have to tell him I couldn't go anywhere with him. With tears streaming down my cheeks, I cupped his face between my palms. At seventeen, he was all grown up, nearly a man and definitely no longer a child.

"I can't leave. But you're right, you don't want to get caught. I need you to get out and run and never come back. I never told them about you. They don't know you exist and that's the only thing keeping you safe."

He wrapped his palms around my wrists but didn't pull my hands from his face. "What do you mean you can't go? We can climb out the window, the same way I got in, and run. I'll help you."

I sucked in a breath as I pushed down the rising emotions clogging my throat.

"Trust me, I want nothing more than to climb out that window and run and I wish it was that simple, but it's not. He put a shock collar on me. It'll zap me if I leave the house."

Even in the dark I saw the flare of fury in his gaze. "He put *what* on you? A fucking shock collar? Like you're some kind of animal."

He whisper-growled the words while he pulled my hands from his face and moved to run his fingers over the collar. I let him work out for himself what I already knew. There was no taking it off. I'd examined every inch of the damn thing looking for how to get it off but hadn't ever been able to work it out.

The sound of the door handle turning had my blood running ice-cold. I shoved Todd toward the window.

"Go! Run! Hurry!" Why wouldn't he move! "You have to go. You can't save me!"

Light flooded the room. As I blinked against the sudden brightness, Phil grabbed Todd, wrenching an arm up behind him and wrapping a fist in his hair to immobilize him.

I reached for Phil's hands, trying to pull them away from Todd. "Please, let him go! He'll leave and never come back, I promise! I'll do whatever you want, just please let him go!"

Godfrey stepped up beside Phil. With a dark chuckle, he pulled the remote from his pocket and hit the button. I screamed out in pain as I hit the floor in agony while electricity bounced through my body. I was still jerking when he kneeled down in front of my face.

"Naughty girls don't get favors, Martha. You know that. And not telling me about your brother was very naughty of you. You had to know I'd want to know all about him."

He stood and I reached for his ankle, trying to keep him from Todd, but he moved too quickly for me to get a hold of him. Not that it would do any good even if I could get a grip on him. He'd either kick me or zap me again. I watched in horror as Godfrey walked up to Todd, who was trying to break Phil's hold, and punched him at full force in the gut, knocking the wind out of him. Phil released his hold and Todd fell to the floor.

"No! Leave him alone!"

Both men began kicking my baby brother and with every blow they landed I screamed for them to stop but they didn't even slow down. Begging and pleading, I crawled over to them, trying to get between them and him so I could put my body over Todd's. I'd happily die to save him if that's what I needed to do. As soon as I was laying over his motionless body, they stopped the beating.

"Let this be a lesson, Martha. You do not keep secrets from me. The price is death to someone you love."

Sobbing, I clung to Todd. This was more than I could take, and my soul splintered apart as Godfrey dragged me from my brother's body and Phil lifted him and took him away. I tried to follow but Godfrey had a firm grip on me.

"No, you don't. You're going to stay right here. Todd will die and that's on you. First you didn't tell me about him, then you tried to escape with him. I guess the shock collar isn't enough of a deterrent to keep you in line anymore."

Phil came back, blood smeared on his shirt. In his hands were cuffs and canes. A shudder ran through me as Godfrey tore my clothes from me, then I didn't feel anything else. My tears dried on my cheeks as I became completely numb to what was going on around me. Both emotionally and physically.

They'd finally done it. Murdering my innocent, sweet baby brother had broken me completely like nothing else they could have done.

Wednesday 18th October 2017
Martha/Tabitha
"Come here, Martha."

On silent feet, I moved to stand before Godfrey as he pulled something from his pocket. I didn't even try to see what it was; it didn't matter. I was dead although I still breathed. Nothing mattered anymore. Hadn't for the past five months since Todd had been murdered in front of me.

"Hold up your hair."

I did as I was told and continued in my emotionally numb state as he unhooked the shock collar then instructed me to release my hair. Something deep in my mind twitched with life, that this was something I should be reacting to, the feel of air against my neck after so long, but I just couldn't muster any energy to care.

"We have you completely cowed now, do we?" he asked.

Staring blankly at the wall in front of me, I said nothing, did nothing other than blink and breathe. No matter how much I willed my heart and lungs to cease working, they kept going because, apparently, I wasn't allowed to escape this hell even through death. After they murdered Todd, I'd stopped eating, but as soon as Godfrey had noticed that I was losing weight, he began forcing me to eat, alternating between beatings and electric shocks whenever I tried to refuse.

"We're moving today into a home with another girl. I've finally found my Mary to join my Martha." He moved to stand in front of me, into my line of sight so I was now looking at his face. He looked smug, like he'd reached some goal he'd been aiming for.

I didn't care. Nothing mattered.

"You will not speak to Mary. If I catch you saying anything to her, you will be strung up and beaten then put through training. Mary will also be trained then sold. But there will be no going to the auction block for you. You'll be left tied up and naked. I'll have you beaten and trained every day for a month before you'll be allowed to return to your normal duties. Do you understand me?"

I nodded because he seemed to need a response, but he frowned, so maybe I should have shaken my head, not nodded.

"Your lack of reaction has me wondering if you don't believe me."

"She believes you just fine." Phil came up behind me, shifted my hair to the side, then wrapped his palm around the front of my neck, over the flesh that normally was hidden behind the collar. He applied enough pressure that it made breathing difficult and my body shuddered. "We've just broken her spirit enough that she's nothing more than a rag doll for us to play with. Which is mighty convenient, considering the afternoon she's gonna have."

Godfrey shook his head and turned to leave. "Bring her out to the car and let's get going. I want to get her settled into the new house before Mary finishes work and we have our meeting with our new friend."

Phil leaned in and nipped my jawline. "Need to break in the new house properly with our little fuck toy before our new friend finds out about her."

For a moment, I wondered about who this new friend might be, but I easily pushed the worry aside as Phil released my throat, took my arm, and guided me out to the car. There wasn't much they hadn't already subjected me to, so I rarely feared anything they threatened. It was nothing new. Physical pain was all I felt now. My emotions were dead, completely numb.

I kept my head down as I was led to the car. I didn't want to see the outside world I was no longer a part of. Once in the vehicle, I stared at the headrest in front of me and continued to refuse to look at anything outside, no matter how many times Phil or Godfrey tried to entice me by describing various things.

Once we arrived at the new house, everything followed the same routine it always did when we moved location. Godfrey would reset the boundary on my collar before refastening it. Then him and Phil had their fun "breaking in" the new place with me before I was shoved toward the kitchen to start making whatever meal was next.

This location was different to all the others because there was a woman already living here. She hadn't been here when we arrived, but when she did arrive, I was surprised to see how old she was. Godfrey had called her a girl, but she was around my age, and very sweet. She tried to strike up a conversation with me a couple times but I'd shaken my head and slipped away. I didn't care about Godfrey's threat to me, that was nothing new, but I didn't want this sweet woman to be put through training, although I didn't doubt that would be her fate eventually, regardless of what I did, now that Godfrey had her. Unless they intended for her to replace me, and I was the one in for something new.

Chapter 5

Rocky Gully, Texas
Godfrey

Excitement hummed through my blood as the doorbell chimed with my visitor. We'd been planning this meet for a few weeks now. He'd refused to come up to Riverton, but was happy to visit Rocky Gully. That made no damn sense—the towns were only an hour or so apart—but the man had something I wanted desperately so I played his game. And I was sure once he saw Martha, he'd give me whatever the hell I wanted.

Although, I wouldn't be handing her over to him. I'd just found my Mary to match my Martha and I wasn't breaking up my perfect pair of girls, but I was more than happy to let him spend time with her here.

That had me grinning. I'd be videoing those visits to use for blackmail later on.

Phil came into my office with Volt by his side. The drug dealer who'd supplied Martha's stepfather with drugs and had wanted her in payment. This man standing before me was the reason she came running in my direction in the first place.

I rose from my desk and moved around it to shake his hand.

"Welcome to my new home, Volt. I'm so glad we could finally line up our schedules."

He frowned. "You're a fucking priest? Is this a set up?"

I chuckled. "I'm the pastor of my own little church. It's a great way to draw in victims. You're safe here."

He nodded and I indicated the lounge chairs in front of my desk. "Won't you come have a seat. Would you like a drink?"

He shifted to sit while shaking his head. "Maybe later. You wanted to know about Oblivion. I'd like to know how you found out about it, and me."

"Tell me about this new drug you and your cousin created, and then I'll tell you why we've been watching you for the past several years."

He rose to his feet. "No way. That's not how this works. This drug is my ticket to the big time. I'm not risking it on some nobody conman."

"Do you remember a young woman you wanted back in 2006?"

He paused before moving toward the door and frowned my way. "You talking about Tabitha?"

I nodded. "She's in this house. When she ran from you, she ran into me. I should thank you. She's been" —I paused, searching for the right word— "a delight to have with me all these years."

Volt's shoulders straightened as he tensed. "You're

lying. No way would you have that woman here."

"Tell me about this drug, and I'll have her bring you a drink."

He glared at me before he returned to his seat.

"Oblivion is a new drug, beats anything else around like it. It makes the victim crave sex. They have to fuck to sate the need that rises up within them. They have no choice—they'll be in agony if they don't. It removes inhibitions, and best of all it takes their memories. The muscle memory learned is still there, so say you teach your woman to deep-throat a cock, she'll remember the how, but she won't remember the actual training."

"So, the perfect drug to train women for trafficking and prostitution then."

He nodded with a broad grin. "Exactly."

"Did you bring some with you so I can see it in action?"

He shrugged. "Of course I did. It's a liquid that can be mixed into a drink. Completely tasteless. The victim is clueless to the fact they've been drugged."

"How long does it take to work?"

"Not long at all, a few minutes. You'll know when it's kicked in because they'll get hot and will start stripping to cool off."

I nodded and turned to Phil. "Tell Martha to bring us a round of drinks. Once she's come in, please go get Mary for us."

He smirked and rubbed his hands together. "Of course. Coffee, tea, or whiskey, Volt?"

"Whiskey, thanks."

Phil turned to leave, and Volt cleared his throat. "You said you'd have Tabitha bring the drinks."

"Tabitha is now called Martha."

He chuckled. "Like the biblical Martha and Mary. Let me guess, you have Tabitha do all the work while Mary sits at your feet and worships you?"

I smirked. "Well, that's the plan. Martha is now well trained but today is the first day I've had Mary under my control so she's not there yet. I want to get Martha in here and settled before we bring Mary in and give her the drug."

A few minutes later, Martha came in through the door. Phil took the tray from her.

"Go over to the couch," I said. "I think you'll like our new friend."

Phil laid the tray on the coffee table and went back out, to go get Mary. In her lifeless way, Martha moved closer. The incident with her brother had changed her, dulled her light which I wasn't happy about, but it also meant she always did everything she was instructed to, which was damn nice. I stood and gripped her arm, pulling her in against my front as Volt stood and turned.

"You remember Volt, don't you, Martha?"

Her body jolted like I'd hit her in the stomach and she tried to move away. It was the first time she'd reacted to anything since that night with Todd.

"Hello, Tabitha, eh, I mean Martha. Fancy seeing you again after all these years." He shifted to stand directly in front of her but looked to me. "May I touch her?"

I smiled at him. "You can if you're happy for it to affect the price I'm going to pay."

He nodded, "Of course. Once you see how well it works, we'll discuss terms."

He leaned forward and ran a fingertip down the center of her face, neck, and chest, stopping between her breasts.

"Hmm, I've been waiting a long time for this. I want her to sit with me. You can have whoever this other girl is."

I thrust Martha forward into Volt's waiting arms. He buried his nose in her hair before he moved to sit with her settled beside him.

Not wanting to cede control to Volt, I made it clear I was in charge. "I want to drug Mary first. Once she's under the thrall, we'll move forward."

"Fine, fine." Volt was all about Martha, eyeing her as though he could strip her bare with his gaze, and the fear in her eyes had my cock twitching to life. It was good to see she had some life left in her after all. Today was going to be a damn good day.

"This is her tea," I said, indicating the tray on the coffee table. "If you'd add Oblivion, I'll call for Phil to bring her in."

Slipping a hand inside his leather jacket, he pulled out a vial. In plain sight of a wide-eyed Martha, whose face drained of color as her gaze stayed locked onto Volt's hand, he poured it into Mary's tea.

I stood to open the door, revealing a grinning Phil standing beside Mary, who stood with her hands clasped in front of her and a sweet smile on her face. She always looked so damn innocent. It was enough to make any man want to dirty her up a bit.

"Hello, Mirabelle," I said, smiling at her. "I'm so glad you could join us. Please, come have a seat and a cup of tea before we move onto business."

Still smiling, she stepped forward and with a hand on her lower back, I guided her over to the couch. Anticipation of what she'd be doing in the near future had my cock throbbing.

Friday 7th September 2018
Martha/Tabitha

Volt coming back into my world had added a new layer to my hell. The other men had mostly stopped coming to me since Todd's murder as I didn't react to anything they did to me. But Volt had never forgotten about me and his desire for me had built over the years. He was insatiable, coming to the house almost every day to have his fun with me.

I was part of the price Godfrey paid him for his drug that he now used on all his victims other than me. They'd dosed me up with it that first day, but only after they forced me to watch Mary succumb to the drug. She'd gone from sweet and innocent to sex-crazed in minutes, stripping off her own clothes, saying she was too hot to wear them. As soon as Godfrey pulled his cock out, she was on him, sucking him down like she'd been waiting for the opportunity. He'd turned to me and told me next time he'd have me clean the office while she did it, to really be his Mary and Martha, but that wasn't on the cards for that day. Not with Volt there wanting his pound of flesh from me.

They didn't bother mixing the drug into a drink to hide it, but simply forced me to take it straight. I have no memories of what happened next for which I'm grateful, and from how Mary acted afterward, I guessed she had no memory of what had happened either. Sometimes when Volt came, he'd give me the drug but mostly he wanted me aware and able to remember what he did to me.

Seeing Volt that first day had put cracks in my numb shell and forced me to feel things again. I craved the numbness to return but couldn't seem to get to the deep level I'd reached prior to that day. I certainly wasn't back to my previous self. I was still silent, refusing to talk unless I absolutely had to, and moved around as quietly as I could. Self-preservation kept me trying to avoid the notice of Godfrey and his men. Volt was the only one who looked for me specifically. The rest of them seemed to be happy with anyone they could get.

Since moving to this house, Godfrey had rarely reached for me. He either spent his evenings in the basement when he had a new victim, like tonight, or he'd join the others with Mary. Mary was drugged every night with her evening cup of tea before bed and at least a few of his men went with her to her bedroom afterward. That was one reason I chose the evenings to vacuum the downstairs. I didn't want to have to hear them up there with her.

It had been because I was vacuuming that I caught Phil bringing in an unconscious woman earlier. He'd taken her down to the basement and I shuddered at what that woman was in for down there once she woke up. I pretended like I'd seen nothing and kept with my cleaning.

Even when a loud roar started outside and got louder, I kept my head down and the vacuum moving over the carpet. Whatever that noise was, it was outside where I hadn't been allowed to go in too long to remember. However, when the sound came to a stop right outside the house, I paused and frowned at the door. What on earth—

Before I could finish the thought, the front door came crashing open and a large man filled the doorway. He was huge, easily the biggest man I'd ever seen. As he entered, several other rough-looking men followed him, all coming straight for me. The big one grabbed me, scooping me up against his chest. He turned toward the door, moving to take me with him back outside. Panic had me tensing and clearing my throat, trying to get my voice to work.

I had no idea how high Godfrey had set the voltage. He

told me he'd turned it up since Volt came, that if I tried to leave, it would leave me with brain damage and they'd still use me no matter how fucked up I was.

"No! I can't leave." I tried to push myself out of his arms. "It'll hurt."

Someone called out, "Tiny, hold up. Keys! Get over here."

The big man stopped. He set me back on my feet and I reached for my throat, grabbing at the collar, trying to pull it off even though I knew it wouldn't do any good. Freedom was right there, so close I could taste it.

It was too dark outside to see much but I could make out all the bikes and vans, could smell the air was tinged with exhaust from all the vehicles. More men passed me, spreading out through the house, but I kept my gaze focused outside until another huge man caught my attention.

He looked like a Viking warrior of old. Tall with broad shoulders, he had his blond hair braided to form a mohawk. The sides of his skull were clean shaven, and he had a short beard that surrounded his lips pressed into a firm line. His ice-blue eyes were locked onto me and they sparked with fury. I tried to step back away, but I was surrounded by the men and unable to escape.

Even trapped like I was, I couldn't tear my gaze from the Viking. He was furious about something, but even pissed off, he was beautiful. Every single one of Godfrey's men had been clean cut and well-polished. I'd learned not to trust anyone who looked like that.

But these men were nothing like them. The Viking in particular, had a roughness to him that appealed to me. I wanted to touch him, to see if he was real, but I didn't want to risk raising his wrath. Didn't want him to hurt me like every other man I'd met these past years had. But hope flared that if I could get this man on my side, I might just be able to get out of here. He was a warrior, huge and strong. He'd easily be able to crush Godfrey and free me, if he chose to do so.

Chapter 6

Arrow

Nothing should surprise me anymore, but the fact that this woman was staring up at me like I was her fucking knight in shining armor or some shit had me shaking my head in disbelief. She wore a fucking shock collar. For real.

Keys called out, pulling my attention from her to him. "Arrow, go grab my tool kit. Don't you worry, honey, we'll get this thing off you and you outta here. You'll never have to see that piece of shit again, I promise."

Her gaze left me and bounced between everyone standing around her. Tiny was still holding her upright and I suspected that was the only thing stopping her from hitting the floor in a heap.

I turned to jog out to the tank to get his gear, not wanting to leave the woman but we had to get that collar off her. I returned in time to hear her tell Keys that Godfrey was in the basement.

Needles took off in that direction. Godfrey had his woman, which was why we'd come in the first place. But now I found my focus had shifted from Bess to this little thing wearing the collar.

Keys nodded in the direction Needles had gone. "Tiny, go with him down there. Arrow will help me here."

Hell yeah, I'd help. My fingers itched to touch her, to hold her and keep her safe. I had no clue why, but this woman brought out my protective streak like never before. Tiny gently guided her to me and I took over holding her up with a firm grip on her upper arms, with her facing me, so Keys could get to the back of the collar. He pulled some lock picking tools out of his bag and got to work.

"We'll have you free in no time, *engill*."

She was back to staring up at me. I was over a foot taller than her and I wasn't sure I'd earned the hero worship she had stamped on her expression, but I'd take it over the fear she'd had in her gaze earlier.

"What's your name?" I asked.

She licked her lips and frowned, like she wasn't sure. But before I could ask her again, a commotion erupted upstairs. She stiffened and turned as my club brothers shoved two naked men down the stairs. They'd clearly taken a few shots at them already and once at the landing, they grabbed them and dragged them outside, calling for zip-ties. A choked sob left my girl's mouth as Mac came down carrying a woman who was writhing against him, clawing at her clothes and him, as though she was trying to get naked and wrapped around him.

"Fucking bastards had her up in that room doing shit that ain't natural," he said. "Gonna need Donna to see what she can do to calm her down. They've fucking drugged her up on something foul."

"Oblivion."

I barely heard the whispered word but before I could ask her what she meant by it, Keys had the collar open and leaned forward to lift it from around her neck. The second it was free, she reached up and covered the revealed skin with her hands, as though she needed the physical proof to believe she was free from it.

Needles came from the basement with his woman in his arms and paused beside us.

"You find the other girl yet? The one that used to own this place?"

Keys answered as he packed up his tools. "Yeah, they've got her out in the yard. She was in a room upstairs with his two men. Fucking bastards. She'd been drugged up on some fucking thing. House of fucking horrors is what we've stepped into here."

That was right. Who knew what else we were going to find in this place before the night was done?

"It wasn't Bess he was working over. He was making her watch while he did it to a fucking boy first. Kid's gotta still be in his damn teens."

My girl jerked away from me and lunged to grab Needles' arm in a tight grip. "A boy was down there?"

Her voice was still quiet, rough, like she hadn't said much in a while, but it was getting smoother the more she spoke.

Needles cocked his head at her. "Yeah, you know who he is?"

She shook her head and when I moved to her side, I could see her eyes were filled with tears now.

"I hope not," she whispered.

Before I could guess her intention, she bolted toward the basement. Without thought, I took off after her. She didn't need to see whatever was going on down there.

Unfortunately, she was damn fast, and I didn't catch up to her until she was flying down the stairs. The moment she hit the basement floor, she stopped and the sound that left her was barely human. The chilling sound silenced everyone who was working on freeing the bloody body of the teen from the chains that bound him to a bench. Hell, it even stilled Godfrey who'd been trying to break free of Tiny's hold on him.

When she went to move again, I wrapped an arm around her waist and pulled her back against me.

"No, *engill*, they've got him covered," I said. "You don't want to get in the way."

Fuck, I didn't even know if the kid was alive.

"Todd…"

She groaned out the name and tried to push my arm away from her.

"You know who he is?"

Her gaze was still locked on the boy's body. "My brother. He's my brother."

Scout growled in our direction. "Get her outta here. He's alive but we gotta get him out to Donna."

With a nod to Scout, I scooped up my girl and raced back up the stairs, ignoring her thrashing as I got us out of that basement. I stopped short when I entered the hallway to discover several of my brothers had guns trained on me. Her scream had been enough to have everyone on high alert.

"It's her fucking brother down there."

She twisted in my grip, trying to claw free of me to go back to her brother.

I tightened my hold as I tried to get her to settle down. "You can't go back down there. We'll stay here until they bring him up. That's the closest you'll get to him until we get him settled in the ambulance. Let the men get him loose."

She didn't stop wriggling and trying to get free, but I had a good grip on her and kept her in my arms. When Scout came up the stairs, the boy in his arms, my girl let out a broken sob which had the boy looking her way. His eyes locked with hers and she reached for him. I shifted close enough she could touch him, and she stroked his face.

"I'm so sorry," she whispered.

The boy winced. "Not your fault."

"Time to move out."

Scout put action to his words and strode toward the front door, me right behind him with my girl, who was still trying to break free from me even though I was taking her where she wanted to go.

This was going to be a long fucking night.

Tabitha

"Stop fighting me, *engill*, I won't be able to let you go in the ambulance with him if you're thrashing around."

I stilled at my Viking's words and instead clung to his leather vest as he lowered my feet to the ground, keeping his thick arm around my waist. I twisted around to keep an eye on Todd. The man who'd carried him from the basement had laid him on an ambulance gurney. When a woman approached with a needle, I tensed up.

"What are they doing to him? He's suffered enough!"

"Shh, *engill*, they're giving him pain meds. Need to get him stabilized so we can take him to hospital."

Sure enough, a minute later, Todd's body relaxed as he slipped into unconsciousness.

I turned to look up at my Viking. "Please, I want to go with him."

He looked down at me, his ice-blue eyes catching my attention fully.

"You promise to not interfere with anything Donna needs to do? She's a trained nurse. You can trust her to not do you or him any harm."

"I promise."

I'd promise him the damn moon as long as I didn't get separated from my brother again.

"Okay, we'll wait for them to load him in then I'll take you over. You going to tell me your name yet or do I just keep calling you *engill*?"

"What does that even mean?"

"It's Nordic for angel."

I blinked in shock. "Oh."

No one had said anything so sweet to me in a damn long time.

"I'm Arrow, and this is my club, the Charon MC, that's come to rescue y'all."

I frowned. "Your mother named you Arrow? Like the weapon?"

His lips twitched but he didn't laugh, although I suspected he wanted to.

"My legal name is Bodie, but my road name is Arrow. That's what everyone calls me. It's because I'm known to say shit how it is. I don't play bullshit games."

I nodded. "I have two names, too. I was born Tabitha, but he renamed me Martha. You know? Like the biblical Martha who ran around cleaning and preparing everything while Mary sat at his feet."

His gaze turned cold again. "I can just imagine the fucking fun he had with that. So, what do you want to be called now? Tabitha? Or something completely new?"

I chewed my bottom lip, thinking about it. "I definitely never want to be called Martha again. I'd like to go back to being Tabitha."

Todd was loaded into the ambulance and before I could move away from Arrow, he scooped me back up into his arms and carried me over there.

"I can walk."

"It's safer this way."

I went to ask him what he meant by that, but then he was setting me on my feet in the back of the ambulance and all I could think about was Todd.

The woman who'd been working on Todd, waved me further inside. "Here, sugar. You can sit up here near his head."

"Thank you. Can I touch him?"

He was covered in welts and cuts. I didn't want to hurt him worse.

"Sure, if you're gentle and avoid any open wounds. And stay away from the line I've got going into his arm. Do you have any injuries I need to look at?"

I shook my head, my gaze riveted on Todd as I sat where she'd told me to.

"I'm fine, please, just fix my brother."

She put her hand on my shoulder and I glanced up at her, into her kind gray eyes. "Sweetheart, you're important, too. I'm here to make sure you both get the care you need. Your brother is as comfortable as I can make him for the moment. I can take a little time to check you over, then we'll get going to the hospital where they'll do everything they can to help you both."

"I'm unharmed. It wasn't me they wanted tonight."

Turning back to Todd, I rested my arm on the pillow, curling it around his head before I leaned in to press a kiss to his temple, ignoring the tears tracking down my cheeks.

I swallowed the sob that rose up as I realized we'd actually made it out of there. We were finally free.

From outside came a gruff voice filled with rage. I jerked to look out the doors at a tall man with a big bushy beard. I recognized him as the man who'd carried Todd out of the basement.

"You fucked with the wrong people. You fucked with someone under my protection. The Charon MC takes care of our own. You're about to get a nice, long taste of Charon justice before we send you to the depths of hell, where you fucking belong."

The woman put her hand on my shoulder again. "It's all right, sugar. That's just Scout. He's the president of the Charon MC and he's pissed as hell over what Godfrey's been doing. Him and the others will take care of that piece of shit, and all his men. You won't ever have to worry about them again."

Men were dragging the now-unconscious Godfrey to a van. Phil and Ronald were already sitting in there, looking worse for wear with how their arms were pulled back. I figured they'd both had their wrists tied up somehow, but unlike Godfrey, they were still conscious.

"Don't look at them, Tabitha," she said. "They're not worth your attention."

I flicked my gaze back to Arrow who stood at the

ambulance's open doors along with the man who'd removed my collar.

"You're coming to the hospital, right?" I asked.

His lips kicked up in a small smile. "Sure, *engill*, I'll be right behind the ambulance the whole way. You want me with you at the hospital, that's where I'll be."

I returned his smile, feeling safer knowing this warrior had my back. Because Godfrey had more than those two men, and Volt was still out there somewhere. I couldn't fight them all off on my own. I needed help if I wanted me and Todd to stay free and I was choosing to put my trust in this man and his club to help me.

I wouldn't fail Todd again. I'd take whatever help I could to make sure of it.

"See you in a bit, *engill*."

With that, the men shut the doors and a few minutes later we were heading away from Godfrey's house and on our way to a hospital and a new beginning. The rumble of all the Harleys that surrounded us allowed me to relax, knowing they had us covered. I could barely believe that we were truly safe for the first time in a long while. But I wasn't sure I could—or should—trust that either of us were going to stay that way for long. That just wasn't how my life had played out so far.

Chapter 7

Monday 1ˢᵗ November 2018
Lone Oak Rehabilitation Center, Houston, Texas
Tabitha

Biting my thumbnail, I stood in the corner of the common area of the facility I was living in, trying to blend in against the wall. I didn't want to be out here. I wanted to be in with Todd, making sure he was okay and had everything he needed. I wished we could share a room, but Ms. Mason, the director, had refused that request when the Charon MC had first brought us here after we'd been released from the hospital. One patient to a room was apparently an unbreakable rule. *Damn them.*

I'd spent the morning with him, holding his hand, then reading to him as he lay motionless in his bed. Godfrey had shattered him down to the soul with what he'd done to him. I squeezed my eyes shut as the familiar guilt ripped through me. Everything that had happened was my fault. All my fault. If only I hadn't run that day, Godfrey never would have gotten his hands on either of us. I'd left to avoid Volt, but he got me in the end anyway.

I might as well have stayed. At least that way I'd still have Todd, and maybe even Mikey might have come good with time.

I glanced down the hallway again, toward the door that blocked me from Todd's room. Dr. Stringer was the doctor assigned to both me and Todd and she was currently in with him. I hated that I wasn't allowed to be in there with them. At least when we'd been back at Bridgewater Hospital after we were rescued, the nurses had put us in a room with two beds, so I'd been able to keep him in my sight at all times. While my Viking and his friends had kept us both in theirs, making sure we stayed protected.

"Tabitha?"

Holding my body still, I shifted my gaze to Mirabelle who'd moved to stand beside me. She had her arms crossed and was rubbing her palms up and down her arms. I wasn't sure who had it worse, me or Mirabelle. She'd been drugged with Oblivion regularly, so even though she now knew what had happened to her, she had no memory of any of the abuses. I, on the other hand, could remember so much of it all.

When my silence and stillness didn't have her moving on, I realized I was going to have to talk to her to get her to leave me alone.

"Yes, Mirabelle?"

"I, uh." She exhaled deeply, tears gathering in her eyes, making me panic and want to run far from her. "I'm sorry. I had no idea you were being held against your will, that the necklace you wore wasn't just a piece of chunky jewelry. *Gah*, I feel so stupid that I fell for all his bullshit."

She looked up, blowing out another breath as she dashed the tears from her face. Her words broke through my shell enough that I peeled myself from the wall and turned to face her.

"He caught us both the same way. We were young and way too trusting, and he was charismatic and used our naivety against us. He drew us in, and we only saw what he wanted us to see. It's human nature to not look beyond the surface."

With a shake of her head, she gave me a watery chuckle. "Guess that answers the question on whether you listen to Dr. Stringer or not."

I shrugged, feeling my cheeks heat. "Something was bound to sink in eventually, right?"

Mirabelle gave me a small smile. "I wish I'd taken the time to talk to you more before."

I shook my head. "It never would have happened. I wouldn't have let you. Godfrey made it clear what would happen if I we were ever friendly with each other. I stayed away from you to protect you."

She frowned. "Protect me from what? He was already drugging and abusing me."

"But he didn't sell you off on the auction block. That drug was a gift. The fact you don't remember is a blessing."

A wince tightened her features. "It's coming back. In

my dreams, nightmares. I see snippets of things that happened. And the drug has messed with my mind. I forget things all the time. My short-term memory is shot. It's no blessing, either way. Do you know what happened to him?"

Reeling from what she just said, I answered without thought. "Arrow said we never need to worry about him again, that we never have to see him again. I take that to mean the club did what motorcycle clubs do best. They've disposed of him somehow."

Mirabelle nodded. "I'm glad we don't have to go to court and go through all of that crap. I hope they killed him and that he suffered for a long time before they did."

With that parting remark, she turned and walked away, leaving me to try to process the harsh words that had just come out of that sweet girl's mouth. Then it was my turn to dash away tears. Mirabelle had been the kindest, most innocent woman I'd ever met. Despite the fact we'd not spoken, I'd noticed how she spoke to others and treated them. She'd been almost childlike in her view of the world. Godfrey had delighted in defiling her while she was high on Oblivion, then switching to being her mentor and friend when she wasn't.

I, too, hoped the Charon MC had made that fucker suffer for a good long while before they sent him to hell.

Arrow

As the club treasurer, I handled a lot of the paperwork. Being the club secretary, Keys helped out, but since I was in charge of paying the bills, a lot of shit came straight to me to deal with. Like the reports from the Lone Oak Rehab Center in Houston where Tabitha, Todd, and Mirabelle were currently residing.

I made sure I got a good look at those when they came in each week. While all three of them had been through horrific abuse, it was Tabitha who held my attention the most. Each report was basically the same. She didn't care about herself at all, just her brother. All she wanted was for Todd to recover.

The woman had no self-worth left, because that bastard Godfrey had stripped it all away. I'd seen the timeline of events. She'd met Godfrey in 2006 and for four years was his housekeeper, free to come and go from the house. But in 2010 things changed. I have no idea what happened to cause the shift, but it was then that Godfrey had started to keep her locked in the house. Tabitha hadn't freely moved around outside of Godfrey's various homes since 2010.

Even though she was free of him and his abuse now, she still wasn't free to wander around outside. After the rescue, she'd gone from the hospital to Lone Oaks, where she was still being monitored and controlled.

Filing away the report with the others in the cabinet, I grabbed my keys and headed for the door. I needed to get out of the clubhouse, feel wind on my face. I nodded to the few others who were doing who knew what around the place as I passed them, but didn't stop. Not until I was out by my Harley where I had to pause to grab my helmet from where I'd left it in my saddle bag. Then I was riding through the gates and heading out of Bridgewater. When I hit the highway and opened up the throttle, I could finally take a deep breath.

For some reason, that little slip of a woman had gotten under my skin and inside my head. I couldn't stop thinking about her. Worrying if she was all right. Which was a load of bullshit. No way was she anywhere near okay. That fucker Godfrey had used and abused her for eight fucking years. No one would come out of that normal. Hell, it was a testament to how fucking strong she was that she even survived. I'll never forget the way she looked when Keys unlocked the shock collar she'd been forced to wear. The way her body trembled while she felt her bare neck.

Ripped my heart right open. Then having her in my arms, the way she fit in against me as though I'd been made to fit around her. Fuck. I missed her. I'd gotten her out of that house of fucking horrors and into the tank, then I'd stayed close while she'd been in hospital at her request. But once she'd been transferred up to the rehab facility, I'd stayed away. I didn't want to remind her of that night and hinder her ability to heal and move on.

But she wasn't even trying to do either of those things. She was so focused on her brother that she couldn't even see that she needed help.

Eight years of abuse and she was telling the doctor that she was just fine, that they should be working with her brother. I mentally shook my head. No way was that girl fine. She shouldn't be fine. She should be ranting and raving, angry with a world that allowed such evil to exist. That didn't notice her suffering for so long.

Switching gears, I slowed down as I entered the outskirts of Houston. I hadn't planned on coming this way, but it wasn't a surprise I was heading to her, considering she was all I could think about. Maybe if I spent some time with her, I could get her out of my fucking head for a while and I could focus on something else.

After parking, I winced as I strode up the stairs to the front door. The place was one of the best in the state, and they'd tried to make it look like a private residence. However, the bars on the windows and the medical clinic-like entrance gave it away.

The security guard sitting inside the door stood straighter as I entered. I gave him a head tilt on my way past, not saying a word to the man. I honestly didn't give a fuck what he thought I was doing here.

Going to the front desk, I smiled at the woman sitting behind the counter as I handed over my ID.

"My name is Bodie Trygg and I'm here to see Tabitha Benoit."

She smiled at me while she tapped away at her computer, no doubt checking to see if I was on the list of approved visitors for Tabitha. Since I knew I was, I just waited for her to work it out, before she moved on to logging in my details to the system.

"Did you want to speak with her doctor at all while you're here?" she asked.

I shook my head. "I've read her report. I just wanted to drop in and say hi."

"Looks like she's in the activity room at the moment. Do you know the way?"

I shook my head again. "Haven't been here before, ma'am. If you could give me directions, I'd appreciate it."

She beamed at me, like I'd made her day or some shit because I used some manners.

"Well, sugar, it's real easy. You just head down that hallway all the way to the end," she said, pointing, "and you're there."

I gave her a nod as I murmured a thank you and moved down the hall she'd indicated. As I reached the end, I slowed down. I'd expected the place to smell like a hospital, but it didn't. While it appeared clean to medical standards, the air held a hint of lavender, not antiseptic. I hoped that helped Tabitha and the others feel more comfortable.

I was killing time and I knew it. Mentally kicking my own ass, I stepped into the large room, forcing myself to stop putting off seeing her. I had no clue what I'd say to her, but I'd come this far; I could hardly sneak out and pretend I hadn't come to visit her now. Scanning the room, I couldn't find her.

Mirabelle sat curled up in a chair with a book. Stiffening, she looked up as I focused on her. She frowned and put her book aside before rising. She flowed to her feet in a smooth, silent movement.

Tabitha wasn't the only one Godfrey had fucked up. Mirabelle was an adult, nearly thirty years old, but she was extremely childlike. From what Bess had told us, she'd always been that way. Skipping through life only seeing the rainbows and sunshine. In discovering what Godfrey had done to her while she'd been drugged, Mirabelle had lost some of her shine. According to the reports, she'd been given Oblivion so often it had left her with short term memory problems. Some days I wished the club hadn't killed Godfrey so quickly. That piece of shit hadn't suffered nearly enough.

"You're one of them, aren't you?" she asked.

I tilted my head, looking down at her as she came to stand before me. "One of who, darlin'?"

"The club that rescued us. You were there that night..." Her cheeks pinkened. Clearly, she'd been told about what she'd been like when we found her. High on Oblivion, a new drug we'd had the displeasure of coming across a few times now, she'd been naked and sex-crazed. Two of Godfrey's men were found in the room with her, abusing her, when we'd busted that place open. Like Godfrey, we'd sent them straight to hell, too.

"I am. My name is Arrow. I was downstairs with the ones who helped Tabitha." I hoped letting her know I hadn't been with her while she'd been under the influence of the drug would help her feel less embarrassed about it all. None of it had been her fault. That was all on Godfrey and his fucked-up crew.

"Why are you here? Are we in danger? Is Godfrey…"

Her voice faded, as though her throat had tightened. I wanted to reach out and grab her shoulders, steady her, but I didn't want to freak her out, so I just held up my palms.

"No, nothing like that. Godfrey is gone. Forever. He can't come back." I couldn't tell her outright he was dead, that we'd killed him, but hopefully she wouldn't need that to believe she was safe. "I'm here to see Tabitha. The lady at the desk said she was in here, but I can't see her."

I scanned around again, but still couldn't find her.

"She hides. She doesn't like to be seen, by anyone. If you look in the shadows, you'll find her."

With that, she turned and glided over the carpet back to her chair where she returned to reading her book as though I'd not interrupted her. My heart broke a little more watching her. There was no spark in her eyes, no bounce to her step. This woman held little resemblance to the one Bess had told us about, and I couldn't help but wonder what Tabitha had been like prior to meeting Godfrey.

Chapter 8

Tabitha

When my Viking strode in through the doorway, I pushed myself against the tall bookshelves. The room's windows were all open and the sunlight didn't give me many shadows to hide in but hopefully he wouldn't see me back here in the far corner. The bookshelf was a large, heavy timber one that I often hid beside. I could see the whole room from here, but mostly went unseen by everyone.

Mirabelle walked over to him and they chatted briefly. I couldn't hear what they were saying but clearly, he wasn't here to hurt her. Not with how he raised his palms, or how relaxed his stance was. He kept glancing around the room as they spoke, but he never turned all the way around to see me in my hiding spot.

At least, not until after Mirabelle went back to her chair and he moved to scan the entire room. Closing my eyes, I pressed myself back against the wall and held my breath, praying to stay unnoticed. Damn these times when I couldn't be in with Todd.

"Tabitha?"

His deep voice sent a strange sizzle through my veins, just like it had the first time I heard him. I had no idea what it meant. He'd carried me out of my prison, away from Godfrey, then stayed with me in the hospital, but I'd not seen him since arriving here. That told me how he felt; I was nothing but an inconvenience.

Sucking in a breath, I opened my eyes and instantly got lost in his ice-blue irises. When he blinked, it broke my trance and I ran my gaze over the rest of him. His blond hair was loose and hung down to a little past his shoulders. It looked thick and had a nice wave to it. I wondered what it felt like. Was it soft?

He cleared his throat and heat raced over my cheeks before I looked back into his eyes.

"Yes, Arrow?"

"Dropped in to see how you're doing. Wanna come sit at a table with me?"

Continuing to move nothing but my eyes, I glanced around the room. There were a couple chairs free at a table, but it was next to Mia who would eavesdrop and get in my face about whatever Arrow and I spoke about for the next few weeks. No way was I going there.

I looked to the windows. It was sunny outside. Maybe we could go out there. I'd avoided leaving the building. The outside world was scary.

After following my gaze, Arrow turned back to me. "You want to go outside? We can totally do that. You know I'll protect you, keep you safe."

I chewed on my lip, looking out the glass to the

manicured garden. It did look nice out there. The sound of a chair scraping the floor had me focusing on Mia who'd seen Arrow was with me and was now heading this way. I couldn't let her join us. I'd never hear the end of it.

I gave him a slight nod. "Please."

I forced myself away from the wall, and he slipped his palm around to my lower back, keeping me moving toward the door.

"C'mon, *engill*, let's go get some fresh air."

Even through my shirt I could feel the warmth of his hand and it helped keep me grounded as we approached the door. There were high fences around the garden making it a private little oasis, safe from the outside world.

Taking a deep breath, I pushed the door open and stepped outside. Arrow didn't let me stop walking until we were away from the building and under the big oak tree that was the reason behind the center's name. Once we slipped into the shadows again, some of the tension left me.

He moved to lean against the thick trunk of the oak. "Do you like lavender?"

Glancing around, I took in a deep breath, enjoying the crispness that was so different from the lavender-scented air within the facility.

"I used to, but I suspect now it'll always make me think of this place and what happened to me."

He nodded but his gaze kept roaming the area around

us, as though he was looking for potential threats.

"Aromatherapy can be very effective, but scents and smells can also become triggers. I wondered if you found the lavender soothing or not."

I shrugged a shoulder. "It's better than that fake citrus scent most cleaners have, but I don't think it makes much difference to me. I'm not sure if Todd finds it calming. I'll have to ask him later."

His attention shifted back down to me.

"Do you come out here often then?" he asked. "To get some fresh air."

I shook my head, not moving my gaze from his pretty blue irises. "I've never been out here."

He frowned down at me. "Why not? It's beautiful. The fences are high and look to be completely secure. You're safe out here, aren't you?"

"As far as I know it's safe out here."

It felt safe, but I wasn't sure if that was more to do with the fact that I had Arrow with me, or the high fencing. Breaking my gaze from his, I looked around at the various plants and noticed the ones that were flowering had a few bees buzzing around them. The grass was perfectly maintained, and I curled my toes in my shoes, wondering how it would feel to go barefoot on that thick green carpet.

"Then why not come out here? Surely you get sick of being stuck inside. I know I do. I'd go crazy if I couldn't get out and ride, feel the wind against my face."

The thought of how that would feel made me smile a

little. Riding on a bike. Free.

"I'm not used to it," I said. "I was only allowed outside when we moved to a new location, and then it was only from the old house, to the car, then to the new place."

I didn't talk about my past. I knew that frustrated Dr. Stringer, that I wouldn't let her help me, but I didn't need it. What I needed was for her to help Todd. My brother was what was important.

"Ah, fuck, *engill*. No wonder you stay inside. Well, how about I come for visits more often and help you get used to it out here?"

I nodded, still focused on the lush green grass. Maybe next time he came, I'd be brave enough to kick off my shoes and run over that patch of lawn.

Arrow

The next couple of reports that came across my desk indicated that while Tabitha was still wanting everyone to focus on her brother, she had opened up a little about what she'd personally suffered. She was also starting to come out of the shadows, no longer hiding behind the bookshelf every time she was forced to spend time in the activity room. She still spent a lot of time there, but not all her time like she had been doing.

Thanks to that improvement, I'd gotten permission from her doctor to take her out today. I hadn't missed the look that had crossed her face every time I mentioned riding my Harley, but she wasn't ready for that. For having to hold onto me and be that close to a man. Or anyone, for that matter. So, today's plan was to take her for a wander around Houston. The facility was near Montrose, which was filled with brightly painted buildings and funky shops. Hopefully, it also wouldn't be too crowded for her to handle.

Nitro knocked on the doorframe before he came into my office. "You ready to head out, brother?"

Nitro was a big man, although not as tall as me. He had a closely cropped beard and short hair that was a few shades darker blond than mine. He was one tough son of a bitch and someone I'd happily have at my back any day. He stood with his arm around his old lady, Cindy, holding her close to him. I'd asked if they'd like to join us on the outing. Montrose was a favorite of Cindy's and she had a few suggestions on where we could go within the neighborhood.

I gave him a nod. "Yeah, let's get moving."

The ride into Houston passed in a blur. I was nervous about how Tabitha would react to being out in the world, outside the safety of the facility. I hoped having Nitro, and especially Cindy, with me would help.

Cindy was the sweetest woman. She was a professional roller derby player and ran a retail shop in Bridgewater called Retro Funk. She was a little bit outside of the norm, and one of the friendliest people I'd ever met. I hoped like hell she and Tabitha would hit it off. Cindy would be a good friend to her, long after she left this place.

After we parked our bikes, we headed into Lone Oaks. I'd been coming in nearly every day since that first visit two weeks ago, so the staff knew me now, and the security guard didn't get his back up with my presence like he had that first time.

"Morning, Stacey. I've come to take Tabitha on an outing. Did Dr. Stringer let you know?"

The young admin grinned up at me from where she sat behind the desk. "Oh, yes, she told me. I hope you can get her to agree to go with you. It'll be good for her to see the outside world."

I nodded and after she logged the three of us into the system, we headed through to the activity room. My heart ached when Tabitha slipped to her spot by the bookshelves after seeing us. I hadn't mentioned my plan for today to her, not wanting her to worry herself about it, but maybe I should have at least told her I'd be bringing friends today.

I turned to Nitro and Cindy. "Give me a minute, yeah?"

"Sure, brother."

I strode over to where Tabitha was covered in shadows. "Hey Tabitha, I've got a surprise for you."

Her gaze flicked between me and Nitro and Cindy, but other than her eyes, she held perfectly still. It was unnatural and I hated that Godfrey had cowed her so badly she feared being seen. When she didn't say anything, I continued.

"Dr. Stringer gave us permission to go out. I thought

you might like to go for a walk around Houston. We won't go anywhere you don't feel comfortable going."

Her eyes widened and she shifted her full focus to me.

"Outside? Away from Lone Oaks?"

"Yeah, darlin'. Just a little taste of the outside world. You know I'll keep you safe. I invited my club brother, Nitro, and his woman Cindy along to join us. You'll have the three of us watching out for you the whole time. I promise, we won't let anything happen to you."

I reached to take her hand and when she gripped my fingers, I tugged gently until she stepped out of the shadows.

"C'mon, Tabitha. Be brave with me."

She winced but came with me as I led her over to where Nitro and Cindy were waiting. Cindy was frowning and I followed her gaze to see she was watching a woman who was staring at Tabitha. She was a patient here that I'd seen several times. She was often watching Tabitha, but I hadn't gotten a vibe from her she was a danger to my girl or me. I'd have to ask Cindy later what she saw that had her focused on the woman like she was.

"Tabitha, this is Nitro and Cindy," I said, still holding Tabitha's hand. "They're going to join us today. Cindy used to live in Houston and knows all the best places to check out that are away from the bigger crowds."

Cindy smiled at Tabitha, from where she stood beside Nitro. "Sure do. It's great to meet you, Tabitha. You ready to go or do you need to grab your bag?"

Tabitha chewed on her lip, looking so damn fragile. I

wanted nothing more than to wrap her up in my arms until she knew she was safe and could relax.

"I, uh, don't have a bag or anything like that."

I tightened my grip on her hand for a moment. "Don't worry about any of that, *engill.* I've got you covered for anything you might see that you want. Today is mostly just about letting you begin to explore the outside world."

She nodded slightly and we headed to the door where we went through the process of getting Tabitha checked out on a day pass.

Chapter 9

Tabitha

I could feel Mia's stare burning into my back, but I ignored it as I followed Arrow and his friends toward the exit. Nerves had butterflies in my stomach going crazy by the time we'd filled out all the paperwork. I tightened my grip on Arrow's hand and moved closer to him.

"You're doing great, Tabitha," he said. "It's a beautiful sunny day outside and we're just going to go for a walk. No pressure to do anything more than that, okay?"

I nodded but didn't take my gaze from the automatic door that slid open as we approached. My feet didn't want to move. My mind didn't want to risk leaving the safety of this facility, but I also didn't want to disappoint Arrow, or make him look bad in front of his friends. He might stop coming to visit if I did that.

I didn't want him to stop. I enjoyed the stories he told me about his club and his adventures. He loved nature and often would go off on his own on his bike to camp out under the stars, or to his place down the coast. I dreamed of doing the same thing now. They were sweet, wonderful dreams of freedom and happiness, so unlike the nightmares that had become the norm over the past several years.

Taking a deep breath, I held it in as I forced my feet to step over the threshold and outside. As soon as we passed the shadow of the building, the sun was so bright that it blinded me. It was so much brighter than the shady rear yard and I turned to press my face against Arrow's bicep. His scent of leather and pine surrounded me as I breathed in.

"Ah, shit," he said. "Cindy, you got a pair of sunglasses on you?"

"Sure, here. We'll buy her some of her own if she wants. There's a cute little shop not far from here that sells the best glasses."

"Thanks." He shifted so I wasn't pressed against him anymore but before I could protest, he slipped a pair of sunglasses over my eyes.

"Try now, *engill*. I didn't think about it, but of course the full sun is gonna hurt your eyes. Is that better?"

I blinked open my eyes and through the darkened lenses could see without being blinded by the sun.

"It's much better. Thank you."

He smiled down at me and my heart tripped over itself at how beautiful he looked with the sunlight all around him. The moment was broken when a car passed us, the noise making me tense up and forget all about how pretty Arrow was.

"Right. Well, let's get moving," he said. "We're just

going to walk around for a while, okay? If you see any shops or anything you want to go in to or take a closer look at, just say so and we will."

I nodded and sticking close to Arrow's side, began my first real taste of freedom.

Todd

"I'm so sorry I wasn't here earlier. Are you okay? Did you get lunch?"

Tabitha leaned over the side of my chair and kissed my cheek, like she always did, and I frowned when I caught her scent. She smelled different somehow.

"I got lunch just fine," I said.

I had thought it odd a nurse brought it in to me instead of Tabitha. I'd been worried, but once I took my meds, I forgot about it. The drugs worked to banish most of my thoughts, except the nightmares. When it came to reliving the hell Godfrey had put me through, my mind had endless stamina, it seemed.

With a sigh, she sat down on the end of my bed.

"I shouldn't have gone," she said. "I shouldn't have just left you like that. It was selfish of me."

I sat forward, to see her better. She frowned down at her hands. An ache started in my chest and I slowly moved my fist up to rub over it. I needed to focus. Something had happened to my sister. Something different.

"Where did you go?"

She looked up, eyes wide, like I'd shocked her. Whatever.

"You smell different." I shrugged and settled back into the chair beside the window where I spent most of my time.

Tabitha pressed her nose to her shirt's shoulder and inhaled before she smiled.

"Leather and pine. Arrow's scent." She straightened, with a wince, shaking her head. "But I shouldn't have gone with him. I promised I'd never leave you, and I did. I'm so sorry, Todd. Will you ever be able to forgive me?"

There was nothing to forgive. We were both here at this rehab facility, as safe as we could be. She didn't need to be here hovering twenty-four/seven.

"Who, or what, is Arrow?"

"He's a man. Part of the club that rescued us. He's been visiting me and today he came with another couple and we went out. Like not just into the garden but outside. I walked down the street! Todd, I bought sunglasses, and clothes. Me. Out in the open, talking to people! Well, Arrow did most of the talking, but I talked to his friends. Cindy was lovely. And so pretty with all those tattoos."

She was excited and talking so fast I missed half of what she was saying, but it didn't matter. I hadn't seen her like this since before Mom died. It made my eyes water. I wiped them and she stopped chattering with a gasp.

"Todd? Are you okay? Oh, hell. I shouldn't be babbling on about what I got to do while you were stuck here. I won't do it again. I'll stay here. With you. I won't go out again until you can come with me. I won't leave you behind, Todd. Not ever again."

That ache in my chest flared up again and I knew this time it was my heart hurting. Tabitha needed to get better. She'd suffered so much. For eight years she suffered at that bastard Godfrey's hands, and she'd made headway today. Headway she was cutting off because she was worried about me.

Squeezing my eyes shut, I kicked my own ass. I'd run from my foster home to look for her, to find her and rescue her if she'd been in trouble like I suspected she was. Instead, I'd gotten caught myself and now she was trying to save me. At the cost of her own wellness. I couldn't let that continue. This Arrow man had gotten her outside, helped her to begin to shine again. I couldn't be the one to extinguish that light.

Taking a deep breath, I put my hands on the armrests and pushed myself to my feet. I wobbled a little but managed to catch my balance before I toppled over. All the physical abuse Godfrey had doled out, had caused damage that I'd be living with for the rest of my life.

"Todd!"

Tabitha sprung to her feet and came toward me. I wanted to be the one to go to her, dammit. When she was standing right in front of me, clearly unsure what to do, I reached out, resting my palms on both her shoulders as I looked her in the eye. All things I'd not done since the rescue.

"Tabitha, don't let guilt steal your day. What happened

to me was not your fault. I chose to come looking for you. I chose to not listen to you and run after I snuck into your room that day. Godfrey and his men were the ones who abused me, just like they did you. They are the ones to blame. Not you. Not me. You can't not live because of me."

Tears tracked down her face, so I pulled the long sleeve of my shirt over my thumb and used it to dry them.

"That's more than you've said since the rescue."

Releasing her, I moved to sit again. My legs were weak from lack of use for so long and from not healing right after the beatings I'd suffered. To get better, I'd need a lot of physical therapy along with the psychological stuff.

"Yeah, well, I guess realizing you were sacrificing your life for me gave me the kick in the ass I needed to stop feeling sorry for myself."

Before I realized what she was doing, she leaned over and wrapped her arms around me, hugging me tightly to her.

"Oh, Todd. I love you so much. Please don't go back to how you were. I need you to be better. I can't be better if you're not with me."

I patted her on the back as my skin crawled at having so much of her touching me. My mind flashed images of Godfrey and his goons and I started to shake.

"Please. Let me go."

She jumped back like I'd burned her, but I couldn't focus on that; I was struggling to get my mind back to now.

I was safe. He didn't have me anymore.

"He's dead. Godfrey, that is," she said. "The club took care of him, and Arrow assured me he suffered for what he did. We're safe because he can't ever come back for us."

I nodded and my vision dulled. The screams in my head blocked out anything else Tabitha tried to say and, clapping my hands over my ears, I started to rock. I felt a prick in my upper arm but didn't worry about it. My head was going to explode with the screams. Then things began to slow. My heart rate stopped thumping against my ribs. The screams started to quiet and I could hear Tabitha again.

"He's gone, Todd. You're safe. He can't hurt you. Never again."

He can't get me. I'm safe. Safe.

I repeated the mantra until the darkness rose up and took me into a mercifully dreamless sleep.

Chapter 10

Monday 17th December 2018
Tabitha

Today was a bad day. The nightmares were back, darker than ever. Every night this week they'd kept me from getting enough sleep. I was so damn tired I could barely think straight. Which meant when Dr. Stringer had asked me about the dreams this morning, I'd told her—and completely broke apart into a sobbing mess.

The nightmares had eased off while Arrow had been visiting me. But he hadn't been to see me for three long weeks now. Since one of Godfrey's buddies came and snatched Mirabelle late one night, he'd not returned. Had he been coming here to see her? Using visiting me to keep an eye on Mirabelle? Dr. Stringer assured me she was now safe and living with someone from the club. Maybe, now that she was no longer here, Arrow didn't need to pretend to care about me to see her. I didn't want my paranoia to be true, but I wasn't sure what else to think.

His sudden absence in my world had caused a shift in the nightmares. Now when Godfrey had Todd dragged away before he started in on me, Arrow was there, in all his Viking glory. With his arms crossed over his chest, he stood in the doorway, blocking my exit as Godfrey began his abuse, his ice-blue eyes cold as a glacier as he watched every little thing Godfrey did with zero emotion.

A shiver ran through me and I rubbed my palms over my arms, trying to chase away the goosebumps. Movement over at the tables drew my attention and I froze as Mia rose from her chair and came toward me. I pressed back against the wall, keeping as still as I could, wishing she would walk past me. I didn't have much hope she would, not with how she was glaring directly at me.

Oh, why did Todd have his physical therapy session today? If he hadn't been in the gym room with his trainer, I would have been able to sit in his room with him rather than out here.

Mia leaned against the bookshelf, arms crossed over her chest as she raised an eyebrow at me.

"You still sulking over losing your biker? Knew he wouldn't hang around for long. Not with you being so damn dull and boring."

When she first arrived, a week or so after me, Mia had tried to ask me questions about why I was here. What had happened. When I refused to answer, she'd gotten nasty with schoolyard insults. I quickly learned to avoid her the best I could. We had nothing in common and didn't have anything to do with each other so I had no idea why she was being so mean to me.

I stayed silent and motionless. My time with Godfrey had taught me it was safer to keep still and hidden.

Mia sighed dramatically and rolled her eyes.

"Silent treatment? Really. I thought Martha was the mouthy one and Mary was the quiet mouse. Guess they fucked that up when they renamed you both, huh?"

Ice filled my veins as I stood in stunned shock. Mia shouldn't know any of that. No one had called me Martha since the Charons had rescued me.

"How do you know?"

She grinned broadly at me. "Oh, sugar, I know all sorts of fun things about you and sweet little Mary. Such a pity Greg didn't manage to keep his baby doll. That fucking club screwed up his plans, but don't you worry. Your turn is coming and they're onto that club now. Volt's been planning your homecoming for a good long while, long before the club intervened and took you from Godfrey."

Oh, shit. Mia was a plant. *She* was how Mirabelle had been taken. I remember one of Godfrey's associates had been called Greg Simmons, and he'd often leered at Mirabelle when he'd come to the house. And the crazy bitch knew Volt. My heart raced and my lungs struggled to draw in breath. This couldn't be happening! I was supposed to be safe here. And if I wasn't safe, then Todd wasn't, either.

"Oh, bitch, please. A few words from me and you're having a panic attack? Damn, but Volt isn't gonna want to put up with you like this. You better learn how to control this shit or he'll have to drug you just like the doctors here do." She leaned forward and smirked while she patted my cheek with her palm. "Say hi to him for me. I'll stay here and hey, maybe I can bat my eyelids and hide in a corner until that hot biker notices me next. I promise you I won't let his attention slide elsewhere once I have it."

With that, she turned and marched away, leaving me to hyperventilate all on my own. I needed to move, to find a phone to call Arrow. I had to get word to the club about Mia, to keep Todd safe. I tried to take a step forward but stumbled into the bookshelf, knocking several books off and gaining the attention of the whole room, including two staff who came running.

Gasping for breath, I couldn't speak, couldn't tell them what had happened, which had my panic growing even bigger. They led me down the hallway toward my room. One of them called Dr. Stringer. I knew they'd drug me. If I couldn't get myself under control, I'd end up unconscious and unable to fight when Volt came to get me. But no matter what I told myself, I couldn't stop the panic attack that rolled through me, scattering my thoughts and fracturing my sanity.

Arrow

It seemed to be a trend. Whenever life settled down and

became calm, something would happen and blow that peace sky-fucking-high. We thought we'd killed the beast when we took Godfrey and his men down, dispatching those fuckers and sending them to hell. But it turned out we'd just cut off one tentacle.

Godfrey had so many fucking associates it was nearly impossible to get them all, but that didn't mean we weren't going to get it done. Greg Simmons was one such asshole. He'd somehow gotten into the rehab facility in Houston and snatched Mirabelle.

Thanks to Keys being a paranoid bastard who'd somehow managed to tag her with a small GPS chip, we'd been able to trace her location and go save her. Again. She was now staying with Keys and his old lady, Donna. Surrounded by the club, Mirabelle was getting all the help she needed to learn how to live again. I had to wonder if it wouldn't be better to have Tabitha and Todd here in Bridgewater, too.

I hadn't suggested it because Todd wasn't ready to leave that facility and I knew full well that until he was, Tabitha would never agree to move. Also, I couldn't really suggest a damn thing to her since I hadn't seen her in nearly a month. Not since that day Nitro and Cindy had joined me to take her out and around Houston. When Cindy had made a passing comment that had slammed through me and brought up memories that were best left buried. Needing to make sure that shit stayed where it belonged, in the past, I'd focused on burying myself in work.

Thanks to the club deciding to open a new business, Athena Security, I had a new job that gave me plenty of work to keep myself occupied. I had no clue how Keys had been able to do everything by himself for so long, but those days were over. He was naturally the lead and in charge of Athena Security, but along with a few other club brothers, I'd put up my hand to assist him in keeping those the club considered ours safe. That included Mirabelle, Tabitha, and Todd.

Once Mirabelle had been rescued and that fucker Greg Simmons dealt with, I'd been focused on Tabitha and Todd, looking into any lead I could find from all the information we'd pulled from Godfrey's computer and safe. The Feds were supposed to have done this shit already. When we discovered how big Godfrey's operation had been, Scout had Taz's old lady, Flick, who used to work for the FBI, contact her old boss. He'd gladly taken all the information we found at Godfrey's house and told her he'd make sure it was handled.

Handled, my ass. Looked like they hadn't done a damn thing with the information. Thank fuck Keys had copied everything before he delivered it to them, because now we could go in and get this shit dealt with properly. We'd only handed it over in the first place because this shit went a long way outside our stomping ground here in Bridgewater, Texas. We didn't have contacts elsewhere to get things done, but if the Feds weren't going to handle it, we would find a way to make sure justice was served and any other victims were found and rescued.

I was more than happy to be a part of that crew. But while I'd always been decent with a laptop, I was no fucking expert. I'd paid close attention when Keys gave us all a crash course on using his applications and how investigating shit like this went down. With the long hours I was putting in, I'd already managed to find several names that we needed to follow up and deal with, and I wasn't even halfway through all the shit Keys had pulled from the hard drive of Godfrey's computer.

All the brothers who were working with Athena Security were scouring the information. Keys had divided it into years. I'd taken the year Tabitha had come to live with Godfrey, and this last year. I'd wanted to take the year Todd had fallen into Godfrey's hands too, but Keys refused, saying it was too much. Which was true. We were all discovering so many names, I knew this shit was going to have the club busy for a good long while before we got everything dealt with. Most were related to his human trafficking business, but there was also some drug dealing shit in the mix, too.

I'd rushed as much as possible through the data I had, looking for anything that would relate to Tabitha. I didn't neglect the other victims or associates, but instead handed over those names to Keys to get someone else to dig deeper, so I could keep going. Thankfully, Keys had instructed me to focus on threats to Tabitha and Todd, and if I found anyone who could be a danger to them, I'd make it a priority for the club to deal with. After all, Athena Security needed to stay above board... but the

Charon MC would do what they always had. Serve justice and protect the innocent who couldn't protect themselves.

That order from the boss had the added benefit of me not having to admit to anyone this was personal for me. No matter how much I tried to deny it—to deny her—she had slipped under my guard and I cared. Cared enough to sacrifice my days and nights to get this research done to make sure she was safe.

Earlier today, I'd hit pay dirt when I discovered Edward Brown, aka Volt. There had been a brief mention of the name Volt back in 2006 when Godfrey had first acquired Tabitha, but there hadn't been enough details for me to take it any further. But now that I was into the 2018 data, it had come up again, this time with a full legal name to go with the moniker.

Mr. Edward Brown had grown up in DeRidder, Louisiana, the same town that Tabitha and Todd were from. It hadn't taken me long to read enough of Godfrey's notes to realize this is what we'd all been afraid of finding. Volt wanted Tabitha, had wanted her long before Godfrey got his hands on her. It sounded like she was his obsession. Looked like this fucker had been the drug dealer Tabitha's stepdaddy used and the reason Tabitha had run away from home in the first place.

The downside to Athena Security being so new was that we hadn't had time to find office space yet, so we were working out of the clubhouse. And that meant, especially late at night, that the chance of getting visitors was a risk

I had to deal with in order to get my work done. I was still digging for more information on Volt when someone knocked on the doorframe. I glanced up with a frown to see who was disturbing me.

Chapter 11

Arrow

"Arrow? You in here, brother?"

Nitro came in carrying two bottles of beer. Before I could respond, he put a bottle in front of me and took a seat on the other side of the desk. By the look on Nitro's face, he wasn't going anywhere until he'd said whatever the fuck he'd come in here to say, so I grabbed the beer and took a long pull before I focused back at him.

"Got work to do, brother, so just tell me whatever the hell it is that has you sitting there all broody and shit."

With a scoff, Nitro shook his head and took a swig of his own drink.

"You've been hiding out in here for a fucking month now, Arrow. Enough is enough. That girl doesn't deserve you fucking with her head, not after what she's already been through."

Rage flashed through me, but I pushed it away like I always did. "The last thing Tabitha needs is me hanging around. She's doing better, accepting the help that place is offering her."

He nodded and tilted his bottle toward me. "Only because you got her to. I think Cindy's right on this—"

He stopped talking mid-sentence when I hissed a breath and tightened my grip on the bottle, wishing I could throw it at his head to shut him the fuck up.

"Cindy doesn't know a damn fucking thing about this, or me. Leave it alone, Nitro."

He shook his head. "Can't do that, brother. You're hurting. She's hurting. There's a simple solution."

I stood in a rush and paced the length of the office, wishing I could go hit the road. I needed space. Fresh air.

"You've always held yourself apart. Sure, you do your part with the club, join in on runs and shit. But any family stuff, anything to do with women, you always sit it out or at the least stay to the shadows and avoid as much as you can. Hell, brother, you rarely even use the whores. You're basically a celibate biker, and that shit ain't normal."

Frustration built up within me and I couldn't hold it in another second. With a growl, I turned and put my fist through the wall. Pain flared across my knuckles as the drywall gave way and my mind settled a little.

"Arrow, brother, talk to me. What the hell happened that'd have you running scared from this woman who clearly means something to you?"

Nitro moved to stand near me, but I didn't turn to look at him. Instead, I kept my gaze on the hole in the wall, the rough edges of the drywall smeared with my blood. I clenched and released my fist, focusing on the burn across my knuckles.

"My mother was broken. An addict. In a way, I guess my dad was one, too. She was addicted to drugs and my father was addicted to saving her." I continued to flex my hand, letting the pain ground me. "She beat it for a while. Stayed clean when she got pregnant with me and stayed that way until I started school. Guess she needed something to fill all that free time she suddenly had without me there to focus on. Dad worshiped her, gave her anything she wanted. Treated her like a fucking princess. Still wasn't enough. Neither of us were enough to keep her with us. One day, I got home from school and she was gone. Might as well have taken my father with her then. He spent the next six months looking for her. When he found her... it didn't end well. He dropped me at my grandparents' place and vanished. I wasn't quite six fucking years old."

"Damn, brother."

I nodded and let out a long breath.

"I can't fix Tabitha. I can't be her crutch that she'll decide one day isn't enough. I can't be my father."

"This ain't the same situation, Arrow. Tabitha's not an addict. She was horribly abused but came through it."

Nitro didn't know the half of it. I turned to face him.

"She ran away from home. Her stepfather's drug dealer offered to take her in payment. Tabitha heard that shit and ran. She was nineteen fucking years old. Made her way from western Louisiana to the northern panhandle of Texas. Then ran into fucking Godfrey." I nodded to the laptop, even though the screen had now gone to sleep so he couldn't see anything. "I found the drug dealer's name earlier and have been researching him. He never stopped being obsessed with her and he found her a year ago. He struck a deal with Godfrey."

Nitro winced. "And she ended up right back where she would have been if she hadn't run. Fuck, Arrow. That poor girl."

"That woman has been through hell. She needs to find her own feet, not a crutch. Cindy's comment about how we looked like teens with the way she was clutching my hand had me thinking of my folks. Of the way Mom needed Dad to keep her level, needed me to give her purpose twenty-four/seven. I can't do that—be that—to Tabitha."

Nitro gripped my shoulder and looked me in the eye. "Brother, get that shit outta your head. This situation is nothing like your folks. Yeah, she needs to learn to stand on her own, but she can do that with support. What will destroy her is if you let her rely on you, then you rip that support away with no explanation. Which, by the way, is not like you at all, but exactly what you've done. You're always the one in everyone else's face telling them how it is. So, I'm returning the favor."

Before he could say anything else, Scout came striding in with Keys on his heels. Keys had his laptop open resting on a palm. He only ever worked while he walked if it was urgent.

When neither of them spoke straight away, I lost my

patience. "What the fuck has happened now?"

Scout frowned at the hole in the wall before his gaze flicked down to my busted-up knuckles.

"You two having problems we need to deal with?"

I shook my head as Nitro spoke up. "Not at all, prez. I was just setting Arrow straight on a few things to do with his girl. We're all good."

I flexed my fists and spoke through clenched teeth. "She's not my girl."

Scout raised an eyebrow at me, clearly calling bullshit. "Oh, really? So, I guess you don't give a shit that Tabitha was snatched earlier tonight?"

My body stilled as the world tilted around me. "Sorry, what?"

Scout crossed his arms and frowned at me. "Tabitha was taken from her room at Lone Oaks tonight. I need to know where you stand on it. I thought you'd give a fuck, but from what you just said, I'm not so sure."

If he wasn't my president, I'd be tempted to take a swing at him. "Of course, I fucking care! I was the one who carried that woman out of Godfrey's house of horrors. What information do we have so far? Was it Volt?"

Keys moved to put his laptop down on the desk and take the seat Nitro had been in earlier.

"After what happened with Mirabelle, I set up some alerts on their security system. I was busy earlier so didn't see the email until just now. They took her out a fire escape and the alarm was triggered. I'm sure we'll get a call at some point about her being taken, but I'm not waiting for it. I've got the trace on her tracker running but it hasn't come back with a location yet. Who the fuck is Volt?"

"Edward Brown, aka Volt. He connected up with Godfrey in December 2017, but Volt is from Tabitha's hometown. He was her stepfather's drug dealer." I paused and looked up to lock my gaze with Scout's. "He's the one who created Oblivion."

Scout shook his head. "This drug keeps popping up. I thought Bruce created that shit and when we blew away his set-up, we ended it, but it keeps turning up."

I glanced back at my screen. "I'm still working through the data. Godfrey was thorough with his research on people. Looks like Edward and Bruce were cousins and worked together on it."

"So why didn't he come after us when we took out his cousin?"

I shrugged a shoulder. "Can't be sure, but at a guess? He didn't really mind we took out the one who he had to share the profits with. Godfrey found out about the connection between him and Tabitha and basically used her to pay for the fucking drug."

My stomach churned as I remembered what I'd read. At the life Tabitha had been forced to fucking endure.

Scout proved that he hadn't come straight in earlier but had stopped to listen to my and Nitro's discussion first. I couldn't be too mad with him over it. Until Keys' program spat out her location, we couldn't do much, and

I'd needed the kick in the ass Nitro had given me.

"So, you're saying that poor woman ran away to escape this fucker when he told her stepdad he'd happily take her in payment for his drugs, was brave enough to leave everything behind and start new, only to run into Godfrey and end up in a worse place. Then to add insult to injury, Volt came back, and she was handed over to him whenever he wanted to have her in payment for drugs. The very thing she'd run away to avoid."

I nodded at Scout's summary and Scout, Keys and Nitro all dropped a few curse words. None of the Charons were happy about what Godfrey had been up to, and with each fresh piece of information we found, we grew angrier that no one had caught onto what he'd been doing before now.

Tabitha

I hated how the sedatives they gave me after a panic attack left me waking up all groggy and out of it. A loud siren had my mind clearing, and I realized I was being carried by two people.

A gruff male voice came from the one carrying my feet. "Fuck, she said she'd have the alarms taken care of. Run!"

The small groan that escaped me was lost with the blaring noise as they sped up and my body was jostled like a rag doll. I kept my eyes closed and forced myself to remain limp, hoping they wouldn't realize I was awake. These had to be the men Mia had been talking about who were going to take me to Volt and never let me see the light of day again.

That thought had panic creeping into my mind and I fought it down, trying to keep my mind clear in order to find a way to escape. The alarm was still blaring when they dropped me into what I guessed was the back of some kind of vehicle. It took some concentration to remain faking unconsciousness through the pain of landing so heavily.

Once I heard a door shut, I risked opening my eyes, just a little at first, and when I saw no one near me, I opened them all the way. I was in the back of a minivan with the door right in front of me. My kidnappers got in and slammed their doors. As they did, the rear door lifted up a crack. It mustn't have latched properly and the jolt from the front doors slamming had it popping open and offering me an escape.

The same man who'd spoken before, spoke again. "Hurry the fuck up! We need to get gone."

Before I could get out and run, the van took off. I snapped out my hand to grab the handle and hold the door down. I didn't want them noticing it hadn't shut properly before I could put it to use.

The vehicle turned and streetlights flashed past, filling the van with light more often than not. I cringed, hoping it wouldn't take long for them to stop again. Surely they'd reach a traffic light or stop sign soon and I'd be able to roll out and make a run for it before they looked back to check on me and noticed I was holding the door.

My muscles were still a little numb from the sedatives, but considering they normally knocked me out till morning I was grateful to be awake at all. Thankfully, my kidnappers continued to be preoccupied with fleeing Lone Oaks and didn't worry about me, but that wouldn't last for much longer. Every mile away from the facility we went, the more likely it was they'd turn around to look over me.

Please stop soon. Please let me be able to escape before they get me to Volt.

The men were talking to each other in low voices as the vehicle slowed then stopped. Figuring it was now or never, I shoved the door and was relieved when it soundlessly swung up all the way. Rolling over, I took off the second my feet hit the ground. Ignoring the feel of the rough asphalt against my bare soles was easy compared to what I'd had to endure under Godfrey's care.

I took off down the closest side street, moving onto the smooth pavement of the sidewalk where I could mostly stay in the shadows of the large trees that grew on the road verge. I didn't stop running until I'd made it to a park. I paused in the middle of a clump of big trees to catch my breath and to see if the men were looking for me. I couldn't hear anything over the pounding of my heart while I ran my gaze over all the streets around the park.

A flash of headlights had me fearing the worst. Pressing

my back against a large tree until the bark bit painfully into my back, I lowered my lids but not so much that I couldn't still see through my eye lashes. Hoping that would lessen the chance of anyone seeing the whites of my eyes in the darkness.

I was deep in the shadows and holding completely still; which should have been enough to keep me hidden. The vehicle came into view and sped along the street closest to me. It didn't slow as it passed my hiding spot and continued on its way until it was out of sight.

Blowing out a breath, I squeezed my eyes shut as relief flowed over me. I'd gotten away. I stayed perfectly still as my heart rate slowed and my breath came easier. Unfortunately, without my heart pounding in my ears, I could hear all the other night sounds. The trees creaked ominously, and panic nearly overwhelmed me when a squirrel scurried across the leaves and twigs a few feet in front of me. I followed the furry little guy with my gaze, focusing solely on it, trying to stay calm. When the squirrel ran up a tree and out of my sight, I leaned my head back and stared up at the night sky, counting my breaths.

I was out in the world on my own, but I was okay. I could do this. I was a grown woman. Being out at night was completely normal and I was fine. I just needed to work out what to do next. Where should I go? I had no phone to call anyone, and even if I did have one, I didn't know any of the phone numbers of anyone who'd come help me. Lone Oaks wasn't safe. Mia was there. The bad guys had broken in twice now.

I had to survive this so I could get Todd out of there. He wasn't safe either. Would the club come for me again? They had gone after Mirabelle when she'd been taken. Would they care about me?

An image of Arrow filled my mind, and I opened my eyes to dispel the mirage. He didn't care anymore, if he ever had. He'd been an illusion I'd latched onto because I wanted to believe someone gave a shit. I'd questioned the reality of him more than once over the weeks since I'd seen him last. Like just maybe I had imagined him, and he'd never been to visit me.

A shifting shadow caught my attention. Holding my breath, I watched as the darkness spread from a tree out toward me. It was coming to get me. The night itself wanted to devour me.

I wasn't safe. Being still wasn't going to make me invisible to that darkness that was coming my way like a wave of oil in the night.

I slipped around the tree and started to run again. I didn't know where I was going but I couldn't risk those oily shadows devouring me. With my thoughts spinning and my lungs burning, I ran until I hit a main street. I skidded to a stop when I was bathed in the light from a streetlamp.

The shops looked familiar, and I realized Arrow must have indeed been real, because this was one of the streets I'd walked down with him and his friends.

"Hey, sugar. You okay?"

With a jerk, I turned my head to see a woman strolling up to me. When she got too close, I held up my hand, wanting her to stop.

"Don't touch me."

She stilled but kept her gaze on me. Her dark eyes seemed to see into my soul. I wanted to run from the scrutiny but couldn't get my legs to move.

"I'm not going to hurt you, girlie, but I'm worried someone else might, or already has," she said. "It's damn late to be out roaming the streets on your own in your pajamas. Are you in trouble? Need help?"

Now that she mentioned it, the pain of the cuts on my feet registered as did the coldness of the night air that sliced through my thin pants and shirt. Silently, I ran my gaze over the woman. Her long dark curly hair surrounded her pretty face. She was dressed in tight-fitting dark blue jeans and a funky top that bared one of her shoulders. With her stiletto boots, she looked ready for a night out. I was interrupting her plans. Would she take that out on me? Hurt me once she got me somewhere not so public. She looked too classy to be working for Volt, but maybe he'd gone for something outside his usual in order to catch me.

"I don't know any Volt, but I assure you, I don't work for anyone who'd hurt a vulnerable young woman."

I winced as I realized I must have spoken out loud. My thoughts were spinning so fast, I could barely catch them, let alone keep them contained.

"You see that pink building across the road? Poison

Girl?" she asked.

I nodded, not moving my gaze from her dark eyes.

"My friend works there. How about we head over and get you cleaned up, call your family—" She stopped talking when I took a step back and shook my head. The only family I had was Todd, and he couldn't do a damn thing to help me. "Okay, okay, no phone calls yet. But please, let me help you. We'll get your feet cleaned up, some warmer clothes, a little food. That sound good?"

An engine revving loudly had me jerking my gaze up the street to see the headlights of a minivan coming down the road. My blood ran cold as I dashed into the closest shadows, pressing up against the wall and hoping if that was the vehicle that held my kidnappers, they didn't see me.

The woman called out. "Aw, fuck. Trew? Need you, now."

A man I hadn't noticed moved from the shadows down the street toward me. He was big with short, curly blond hair and I gulped as fear paralyzed me.

His voice was low and soothing. "Shh, darlin', we mean you no harm. Just stay where you are and let us protect you."

He stood in front of me with his back toward me, his larger frame blocking my smaller body from the road completely. The woman stood to the side of him, blocking any view someone inside the minivan might have had as it approached. As the van passed slowly, her gaze followed its progress with a frown. Were they really protecting me, or would she call out?

The vehicle moved past us and the three of us stayed still until it turned onto a different road further up.

"It's not safe out here. Trew, pick her up and get her over to the bar." She looked me in the eye. "Girlie, I got no clue what trouble you're in, but clearly you need help and I'm going to give it to you. Come."

Her voice was steel that brooked no argument. I curled into myself as the man, Trew, scooped me up and held me like a child against his chest. When he started to walk, I wrapped a fist in his shirt, worried he'd drop me.

"What's your name, darlin'?" the woman asked.

"Mar— Tabitha. It's Tabitha."

My stomach churned over the slip. I'd nearly given them Godfrey's name for me. My head was a such a mess. I needed to be back in my room at Lone Oaks.

I shook my head. No, it wasn't safe there. I wasn't safe anywhere. I had nowhere to go.

I pressed my face against Trew's shoulder, hoping by blocking out my sight, my thoughts would stop, but it backfired when I caught a whiff of leather on Trew. It wasn't as strong as on Arrow, but it was enough to make me think of him.

"Are you a biker, too?" I asked.

He stilled for a moment before he continued across the road and toward the bright pink building.

"Ah, no. I don't ride. Why'd you ask?"

"I smelled leather. Made me think of someone I know. Knew." I shook my head again.

The woman spoke again. "Is that who's after you? An MC?"

I looked at her with wide eyes. "Oh no. The Charons saved me, not hurt me."

Before I could say anything else, the woman opened the door to the bar and Trew strode in. The sudden loud music had me slapping my palms over my ears and whimpering. Too loud, too much. I wriggled, wanting to be put down so I could run away.

"Whoa, not yet," he said. "Let me get you to a seat."

I whimpered again as my body started to tremble. A vision of Arrow's ice-blue eyes filled my mind and a broken sob tore from me. He wasn't here and I had no idea what I was going to do next.

Chapter 12

Arrow

Nitro's phone rang and he started out of my office as he answered it.

"Hey, babe, what's up?"

I kept my focus on Keys' screen, waiting for Tabitha's current location to appear.

"Is there any way to speed this thing up?" I asked.

Keys shook his head. "I know, man. I've been working on creating something quicker but for now this is what we've got. It shouldn't be too much longer."

"We've got her. She's safe."

I spun on Nitro as he came back in, his phone still up against his ear.

Scout stepped away from the desk where he'd been watching Keys and moved toward Nitro. "What do you mean?"

"She's with friends. She's safe. Natalie just called Cindy. Her and Trew were heading into Poison Girl—it's a bar—when they saw a woman run out from a side street onto the main road. Since she was wearing nothing but her pajamas, they figured something wasn't right. While they were talking her into going to the bar with them so they could get her help, she mentioned something about the club so Natalie rang Cindy to see if we knew her. What do you want them to do?"

Scout frowned, with his hands on his hips. He was in full president mode, mentally planning out how to get one of ours back where she belonged. "Where's this bar? And is she injured at all?"

"Sounds like her only injury is that her feet are a mess from running around barefoot. Natalie got Trew to carry her over to the bar, but she's scared out of her mind. Not letting anyone close to her. Poison Girl is a dive bar in Montrose. It's not far from Lone Oaks. We actually walked past it with her last month, that's how close it is."

Scout nodded. "Right. Tell Cindy to call them back and get them to stay where they are. We'll take the tank and a small crew up there. I'll get hold of Blade and get him and Veronica down here. They can join you in the tank, Keys. Arrow, I want you and Machete to head straight out. You're on Tabitha, and Machete will be on Todd once you get back to Lone Oaks. I don't want either of them alone until I can sort out something more permanent for their protection." He shook his head. "I'll try calling Lone Oaks, if I can't get hold of anyone, I'll ride up with you and make sure they don't prevent you two from acting as bodyguards. Utter fucking bullshit they've had two patients snatched in under a fucking month. Not acceptable at all. I want those two guarded twenty-four/seven. Understand?"

"Yes, prez."

He nodded. "Right. I'm going to find Machete and raise Blade. They were here earlier but didn't see if they went upstairs or headed out."

I started packing up my laptop as Scout left, his phone already to his ear as he called Blade.

Tabitha had to be so fucking frightened. Natalie was the captain of the roller derby team Cindy was part of, and she also owned a BDSM club in Houston called Titanium. According to Nitro, she was a good Domme. I assumed that meant she'd be caring and gentle with Tabitha, but she could be Mother Teresa and Tabitha would still be freaked the fuck out. She didn't know her, or this other person, Trew.

Considering how much trouble she had walking around the bustling area of Montrose in the light of day, she had to have been scared out of her mind being forced to run around in the dark. A vision of her pressed back into the shadows of the activity room flashed through my mind and forced me to consider the fact she might have actually been more at ease in the night.

Either way, I wasn't going to leave her out in the world on her own. I was glad Scout had ordered me to guard her door because I'd been thinking of doing just that anyway.

"Right. Let's get moving." I nodded at Keys and followed him out to the front room where Machete joined us, and we continued out to the yard. I stashed my laptop in my saddle bag but before I could close it up, Keys was there with a small first aid kit.

"Take this, you'll be first on scene. We shouldn't be too far behind you, but just in case you need it before we get there."

"Better safe than sorry. Thanks, brother."

After slamming on my helmet, I jumped onto my bike and with a glance to see Machete was ready to roll, I headed out. Normally, Donna joined Keys in the tank, an all-terrain vehicle we'd set up as an ambulance several years ago. The damn thing got put to use way more often than we'd like, but I was glad we had it. Donna was home with Mirabelle, who couldn't be left alone yet, so Veronica was stepping in.

Like Donna, Veronica was a nurse and would know how to treat any injuries Tabitha had. Blade was her man and one of the club's enforcers. He was one of the newest members of the Charon MC but he was solid and had already proven himself time and again to be worthy of being a part of the club.

Tabitha

As soon as Trew put me down, I moved to the back corner of the room and found a shadow to hide in. Wanting to be invisible in this strange place, I didn't say a word as the woman who introduced herself as Natalie made a phone call. When she said Cindy's name, I turned my attention fully her way. She was watching me right back as she spoke into the phone.

Did this stranger really know the same Cindy who'd joined Arrow when he'd shown me around? It didn't seem likely.

When she finished the call, she moved toward me and I held my breath, cringing back against the wall, waiting for some sort of attack from her.

"Whoa, I'm not going to hurt you. Are you Tabitha?"

I nodded but didn't stop trying to push myself through the wall behind me.

"Tabitha, I'm a good friend of Cindy. You remember Cindy, right? Brown hair, lots of tattoos, dresses like a 1950s pin up?"

I nodded again.

"I just called her and she's letting the Charons know you're here."

Her phone rang and she took a few steps away from me to answer it.

I shifted my gaze around the room while she talked. It was a dimly lit bar. There was a row of pinball machines and the walls were covered in photos and paintings of women with their boobs out. That seemed like a strange mix but no one in here seemed to mind, nor were they staring at me. It had to be well past midnight by now and the dozen or so people in the bar all seemed to be busy with their own drama and not caring about me, which suited me just fine.

I tensed when Natalie pocketed her phone and returned

to stand way too close to me.

"The club's coming for you, Tabitha. Arrow is on his way."

I let out a deep breath and tears stung my eyes. I shouldn't be so relieved that he was coming. He'd abandoned me without a word, cut me off. Why was he even coming now? Had someone made him?

"Tabitha, I'd really like to have you sit down," she said. "Your feet are bleeding and if you're comfortable with it, I'd like to have a go at cleaning them."

I looked down at my feet and the blood smears I'd left on the floor. My heart rate picked up as I glanced around for the owner of the bar. Whoever it was had to be mad I'd gotten the floor dirty. I was extra glad the other people in the bar were ignoring me.

"Hey, hey… look back at me, Tabitha," Natalie said. "Take a deep breath. You're safe. No one cares about the mess. We care about your feet. There's a table to your right. Can you move over to it and sit down? Will you let me look at your feet, or would you prefer to wait for Arrow? He's going to be a little while. Even rushing, it'll take over half an hour for him to get here."

I frowned as I looked to the table. It was between me and the noisy pinball machines. Even when they weren't being played, they were loud and had lights that flashed.

As though she could read my mind, Natalie moved over and, reaching behind the machine next to the table, she did something that had the lights go out and the machine fall silent.

She shifted a chair out and held her palm to me. "C'mon, Tabitha. You need to get off your feet. Take a seat and I'll get you a drink, some food. We'll just sit here relaxing until Arrow gets here, okay? No pressure. I only want you to be comfortable."

There was something about her tone that had me reaching for her hand and allowing her to guide me to the seat. It wasn't anything fancy, just a simple timber chair and table, but they were solid and surprisingly comfortable. The moment I took my weight off my feet, pain flared from my soles but it was easy to ignore. Compared to what Godfrey and his men had put me through, it was nothing.

Trew came over with a bottle of water and a bag of chips. He waited for me to look at him before he opened it and set it in front of me. "Here you go, sweetheart."

I gave him a small smile before reaching for the bottle and bringing it to my lips for a drink. My throat was parched but I was careful to sip at the ice-cold liquid. Natalie didn't mention my feet again, for which I was grateful. I didn't want anyone touching me. I wanted to be back in my room at Lone Oaks. I knew those walls, knew what was expected of me there.

But it's not safe there anymore.

No, it wasn't safe. Mia was there and she'd made it a dangerous place for me. Was Todd in danger too? Had he been taken as well? Panic welled up. I couldn't check on him. How could I make sure he was okay, that he hadn't been snatched?

Natalie's voice penetrated my thoughts, pulling me back to reality. "Tabitha, look at me. Wherever you just went in your head, is not where you need to be. You're safe. Arrow is on his way."

I looked to Natalie, who had leaned forward in her chair to get my attention. Her eyes were dark, and it seemed as though she saw straight through me. I struggled to get my breathing under control as I kept my gaze locked with hers.

"What about Todd? Is he safe?"

"Who's Todd, and why wouldn't he be safe?"

"He's my brother. I don't know if he's safe."

She pulled her phone out again and called someone.

"Hey, Cindy," she said into the phone, "you know if her brother, Todd, is safe?"

The reply came from the other end, but I couldn't hear it.

"Uh huh. Thanks, babe." She pocketed the phone before she returned her focus to me. "Todd's safe in his room. No one's touched him."

I nodded and took another sip from my water as relief flowed through me. He was safe.

"Thank you."

She gave me a nod before taking a drink from her own bottle of water. I kept my gaze on her, wondering if I could ever be as strong and confident as she was.

Chapter 13

Arrow

I'd never gotten from Bridgewater to Houston so fast in my life. Thank fuck there hadn't been any cops out on the highway. Machete kept up with me the whole way and as I pulled into the parking lot of Poison Girl, he pulled up right beside me.

Taking my helmet off, I spoke to him. "You coming in before you head over to check on Todd?"

He nodded. "I'm with you until we get Tabitha back to the facility. Scout was going to put the fear of God into the director to make sure she took keeping Todd safe seriously until we get there. For now, my job is to watch your back, brother."

"Good deal."

I rushed to the front entrance of the bar. It was nearly closing time and there were only a couple cars in the lot. Hopefully that meant the place was nearly empty and no one had bothered Tabitha while she'd been forced to wait for us.

Shoving the door open I strode in, scanning the entire place for her as I moved further into the room.

As soon as my gaze caught on her, I couldn't look away. She was huddled at a table in the back corner, in behind the pinball machines. Oddly the two machines closest to her were turned off. But even in the dim light, I could see how pale her skin looked. Her brown hair was a mess, and her pajama top was creased and dirty.

None of that mattered. She still drew me to her. There was something about this woman that had me breaking all my rules. It wasn't that she'd been hurt and needed help; the club was constantly saving women and none of the others had ever effected me like Tabitha did.

After watching my parents destroy each other, I swore I'd never put myself in a situation where that could happen. I wasn't the celibate Nitro had accused me of, but I didn't run around fucking anything I could like some of the other brothers. I hadn't wanted to risk making an attachment and wanting more. But here I was. A woman I'd not even kissed yet was making me think things I knew better than to be contemplating.

She stilled in her seat when she saw me and didn't move as I drew closer. Even when I was right beside her, she was as still as a statue. Like she was fucking scared of me.

"Hey, *engill*, I hear you've had quite an eventful night."

"Arrow?"

I turned at my name and focused on the tall woman standing beside me. I had a few inches on her, but she'd tower over Tabitha. Her long, curly hair was down around her shoulders and despite her casual clothes, she had a distinct don't-fuck-with-me aura that had me thinking this must be Natalie, and she'd already taken a liking to Tabitha. Was willing to take me on if she needed to in order to protect the younger, more fragile woman.

I liked her.

"Yeah. You Natalie?"

She shook my hand before she nodded at Tabitha. "She doesn't seem to recognize you. If she doesn't want to go with you, she won't."

I grinned at her. "Is that right? Well, I suspect she's just a little angry with me right now. I've been busy with work and haven't been to visit in a while. But I'm here now and I ain't going anywhere. I promise you, she's safe with me. And we're staying right here for the moment. A few of the others are coming with our ambulance to get her patched up before we take her back to Lone Oaks—"

I stopped talking when Tabitha stood, knocking her chair over. Before she could run, I reached out and gathered her in against me.

"Not alone, Tabitha. You're not going back alone. I'm not leaving you. I'm going to be staying with you. I'll be standing right outside your door making sure you're safe. But you need them to get better. You're not ready to be out in the world just yet."

She trembled against me and it broke my fucking heart. Shifting my grip, I scooped her up in my arms and sat down with her on my lap. She curled into herself but snuck one hand out to grab a fist full of my shirt beneath my cut.

"That's it, *engill*, I got you. We're going to just sit here and relax while we wait on the others. Do you remember a nurse named Veronica from when you were at the Bridgewater Hospital? She's got dark curly hair, a little longer and darker than Natalie's."

Tabitha nodded a little, blinking up to stare into my face.

"She's Blade's woman, and they're with Keys in the tank. The same one we brought to get you that first time. We'll get your feet taken care of, then we'll head back. I've got my bike, so I'll follow on that, then I'll be staying with you for as long as you need me to."

Her eyes filled with tears and a shard of pain stabbed me through my chest. This woman slayed me. I shifted to wipe the moisture away.

"You're safe, Tabitha. With me, you're always gonna be safe."

She nodded again then licked her lips. "It's not safe to take me back."

"Why? Are you worried the ones that took you tonight will return? Because if they do, we'll get them before they get anywhere near you."

She shook her head. "They have someone inside. Someone who tells them things."

Tabitha liked to observe. I was pretty sure if she knew they had someone inside it was because she'd worked out who it was. "And you know who it is?"

She glanced around the table and Natalie held her palms up. "My lips are sealed, Tabitha. I'm here because I want you safe, nothing more."

"Mia threatened me. Yesterday. Told me they were coming for me."

She continued to tremble and I tightened my hold on her, pulling her in closer against me.

"Shh, it's okay. You don't need to say anything else. We'll deal with her, make sure you're safe."

"And Todd?"

I pressed a kiss to the top of her head. "Yeah, *engill*, your brother too."

She pushed her face in against my chest. I glanced over to Natalie who was looking like she wanted to be a part of taking out whoever this Mia chick was.

"We will make sure she's safe," I said. "You don't need to worry about it."

Natalie nodded but didn't say anything. I got the sense Tabitha had another protector in this woman. Considering the trouble that seemed to follow her, I didn't mind at all having someone else who cared enough to help keep her safe.

Tabitha

A sense of Déjà vu hit me as Arrow carried me from the bar toward the brightly lit ambulance. My mind got muddled and I tightened my grip on his shirt as I glanced around, looking for Godfrey and his men being held by members of the Charon MC.

I mentally shook my head. This wasn't the house in Rocky Gully, I was in Houston.

I tried to focus on the asphalt, the bright pink of the bar, the sign that read Poison Girl. Godfrey wasn't here. He couldn't be here. He was dead.

"Shh, Tabitha," Arrow said. "You're safe. Godfrey can't get to you. He's rotting in hell."

Had I spoken aloud, or was he just that in tune with my thoughts?

When he approached the rear of the vehicle, he moved as though he was going to sit me on the gurney but I tensed and didn't loosen my grip on his shirt. He didn't complain or force me. He simply climbed up into the ambulance and sat on the gurney.

The woman wasn't the same one as before, but Arrow had told me that would be the case. I did recognize this new woman. As Arrow had told me, she'd been at the hospital. Her long black curls were distinctive, even pulled back into a ponytail.

She looked up at me as she put on a pair of thin plastic gloves. "Hi Tabitha, I'm Veronica and I'm a nurse. We've met before, at Bridgewater Hospital. I'm just going to take a look at your feet so if you could bring them up and rest them on the mattress for me, that'd be great. Are you hurt anywhere else? Did they knock you out when they took you?"

I shifted so my feet were up on the bed. When they left dirty red marks, I went to move them back down, mortified I'd mucked up the pristine sheet.

"No, leave them up there. Don't worry about getting anything in here dirty. It's all washable. And I promise you, no one will care about any mess."

Arrow hugged me tighter. "Damn straight. We all just want you safe and well."

I nodded but didn't loosen my grip as Veronica set about cleaning my feet.

"I know exactly how you're feeling, Tabitha," she said. "My uncle was a lot like Godfrey, and he did horrible things to me. When my parents tried to get me away from him, he had them killed. So yeah, I know how it feels to be held captive for so long that you can't trust being free."

I stayed silent, processing what she'd told me as she poked and prodded and frowned a couple times as she cleaned out the cuts. The small flares of pain were nothing and barely registered.

"I had a panic attack and was given meds last night," I said. "I was already out cold when the men came in and took me. I woke up as they were carrying me out to their van."

She nodded as she started to bandage my right foot. "How'd you get free of them?"

The fact she understood had me relaxing with her. "They set off the alarm, which wasn't supposed to happen, so they were rushing. The back door on the van didn't shut properly, so I held it nearly closed as they sped out of the parking lot. When they stopped at an intersection, I shoved the door open, rolled out, and ran."

"So brave and very clever. I had help each time I got free. First my parents, then their lawyer got me a new identity and away. But until Blade and the club got involved, it never held. He always came back until they made it so he couldn't."

I rubbed my cheek against Arrow's chest, the stitching on his name patch rough against my skin.

"Godfrey had so many *friends*. I'm not sure they'll ever stop coming."

A rumbly growl came from Arrow, vibrating his chest. "We'll make sure you're safe, *engill*. That's why I haven't been to visit. I've been going through Godfrey's files and tracking down every fucking person he was ever involved with. It's Volt who's after you now, isn't it?"

A shudder ran through me and he tightened his hold on me. Veronica patted my ankle gently now that she was done bandaging.

I whispered my fear. "He won't ever stop."

Arrow shifted me so he could tilt my face up so that I was looking into his piercing ice-blue eyes.

"I won't ever stop protecting you. You understand me?"

Not really. His mixed messages made no sense but I wasn't going to get into it now, so I simply nodded and tried to snuggle back in against him.

The man who'd taken my collar off, I think his name was Keys, stood at the back of the ambulance. "Right.

Arrow, you're gonna need to put her down so we can all get moving back to Lone Oaks."

Arrow leaving me was the last thing I wanted! I tensed and wrapped my hand back in his shirt. I'd released my tight grip as Veronica had chatted with me and I'd grown comfortable with her.

Another club member who'd been in the ambulance when it had arrived earlier, chuckled but I didn't care if he was laughing at me. I turned to bury my face against Arrow, not wanting to focus on the real world at all. Not wanting him to leave me.

"Blade…" Veronica's voice had a tone of warning in it.

"Damn, little dove, I wasn't laughing at her. You know I wouldn't ever do that. I was laughing at Keys thinking Arrow was going to be able to just leave her. Arrow, give me your keys, brother, and I'll take your bike while you ride over with the women."

I didn't move from where I was hiding against Arrow's big body as he shifted to get his keys and hand them over to his friend. I knew I was being ridiculous. A pathetic creature he probably wanted to run away from, but I couldn't help it. He was my Viking. This huge man, with a broad chest and strong arms… I'd never felt as safe as I did when I was in his arms and I never wanted that feeling to end. Although, I knew it would. Arrow had proven how quick he was to leave, and I doubted this time would be any different.

Chapter 14

Arrow

Three days later and everyone was still on edge. There'd been no more attempts to take either Tabitha or Todd, but since the center's director, Lilith Mason, had refused to remove Mia from the facility we weren't letting down our guard any time soon. Ms. Mason had told us that Mia wasn't well enough to live outside the facility, but I wasn't so sure about that. Something fishy was going on with this place and I wished we had somewhere else we could take Tabitha and Todd to get the help they needed.

Lilith Mason's voice sounded as prim as she looked. "You need to leave."

With my arms crossed over my chest, I stared at the director of Lone Oaks. She'd called us into her office here at the center for this apparently urgent meeting. I was beyond grateful that Scout was taking the lead with speaking to her. I had no clue what Keys was doing on his laptop, but whatever it was, it had his full attention. I stood silently at the back of the room, like a tree, both wondering why the hell Scout insisted on us both being here for this and trying not to give in to the urge to hurt this prissy bitch who thought she was so much better than us.

Scout's voice was a lot more polite than I would have been. "Ms. Mason, two women have been taken from your facility in the past month. That's unacceptable, so we've added security to your business. At no charge, I might add. Why would you want us to leave?"

She cleared her throat before holding her head high. "You're making the patients uncomfortable. The staff have asked me to remove you from the premises. Effective immediately."

I frowned as I took in her stance and tone. Something else was definitely going on here. I glanced over to Keys, who remained still fully focused on whatever he was doing on his laptop so no help.

There was a gruffness to Scout's voice now that indicated he was reaching the end of his patience. "I call bullshit on that. My men haven't reported that any of the patients have shown any fear with them being here. A few of the women have looked like they'd like to jump them, but definitely not fear. My men have been completely professional. They've not engaged with anyone, just silently kept guard and made sure everyone is safe. There is no reason to remove them."

An idea hit me and I stepped forward out of the shadows, gaining Scout and Lilith's attention. "Scout? I need to go check on something. Give me ten, yeah?"

Scout turned to give me a nod and I slipped out of the door. Lilith had mentioned the staff wanting us gone. Todd and Tabitha's doctor, Jacqueline Stringer, had seemed supportive of our presence. I needed to track her down and ask some questions. Ultimately, if Lilith wanted us gone, we were gone. She ruled this place and could do as she pleased, but if there was some foul play going on, I wanted to know about it.

I also wanted to find out if we could lure the good doctor away to Bridgewater. With her in town, we could set up a half-way house for people like Tabitha and Todd, and any others we found as we set about taking down all of Godfrey's associates.

It didn't take me long to reach her office. A quick knock and she called out, inviting me in. She was sitting at her desk, a stack of paperwork in front of her. Jacqueline was a sweet woman, with thick brown hair she kept up in a ponytail or bun, and practical glasses on her nose that did nothing to hide the kindness that radiated from her gray eyes. She was a natural-born healer.

"Hi Arrow. Figured you'd be in with Lilith for a while yet."

"I slipped out. Scout can handle her without me for a bit. I wanted to ask you about something she mentioned."

With a sigh, Jacqueline closed the lid on her laptop and leaned back in her chair. "What did she say I've said?"

"She didn't name names, but she said that some of the staff have told her to get rid of us; that we make the patients uncomfortable."

The frown that creased her brow confirmed my suspicions that Lilith was full of shit.

"I don't know who's told her that. As far as I know, we're all happy to have you here. The first day or two, some of the patients—and staff—were nervous having bikers around, but once they realized you weren't here to hurt them, everyone settled and from what I've observed, most of the patients are calmer knowing there's more security around. After what happened to Mirabelle then Tabitha, it's understandable that they don't feel as safe here as they should."

I nodded. "That's what I figured was happening. I have no idea why Lilith is pulling this shit, but we're not going to just abandon Tabitha and Todd. End of the day, Lilith can force us to leave—she's in charge here. But if we leave, we're taking those two with us. They're not safe here."

She went to interrupt me, but I held up my palm to stop her.

"But, we also know neither of them is ready to be thrust out into the world just yet. How attached to this place are you? Because if you wouldn't mind relocating to Bridgewater, we could set you up with your own place there. Tabitha and Todd would be there to start with. Mirabelle could also return to seeing you, although she seems to be settling in well with Keys and Donna at this stage. Also, there'll be more. The Charon MC won't ever stop shutting down assholes like Godfrey."

I stopped talking and let her think. After a few minutes of silence, she took a deep breath.

"I have no idea what Lilith is playing at, but this isn't like her. Something has changed, and I'm not liking how it could play out. Your proposal has my interest, but are you really able to promise me the things you are? Do you have that authority?"

I shrugged one shoulder. "Scout is the president of the club and we take shit like this to the whole club to vote on, but I can't see them turning it down. Especially if we have you on board."

"I'll need to give notice here. I can't just walk out. No matter what Lilith is pulling, I won't abandon my patients with no warning like that. Take the proposal to your club and see what they say. If it's a yes, get Scout to call me and I'll tell him what I need to make it work."

With a grin, I gave her a nod. "Done. And thank you."

I slipped out and headed back toward Lilith's office. When I entered, Scout was still trying to argue her around to letting us stay.

"Ms. Mason, clearly you want us gone and you're not going to budge on it. If we leave, we're taking Tabitha and Todd with us. You have proven that Lone Oaks is not safe for them. When are you demanding we leave by?"

Scout turned to frown at me, and I gave him a quick *trust me* look.

"Today. I need all Charon MC members gone today. You can come and collect Tabitha and Todd tomorrow."

I shook my head. "No way. We're a package deal. Just told you that. The way you're trying so hard to separate us from them has me wondering if you know more than you're letting on about who's after them. Tell me, Ms. Mason, if we give in to your demand, will Tabitha and Todd be here in the morning or will they miraculously vanish overnight?"

Her phone began to vibrate on the desk and when she glanced at it, she stilled before forcing a fake professional smile on her face and looking back to me.

"I have no idea what you're talking about—"

Keys stood as he spoke and cut her off. "He knows more than you think he does. No clue how he figured it out, but I worked it out by hacking into your phone records. That phone call you just ignored is from someone who calls you every day at about this time. Bet they're gonna be pissed you ignored them. Arrow, you seem to have an idea about what's going on. You know who could be behind those calls?"

I frowned at Keys before turning back to Lilith.

"I didn't know anything about phone calls, I just figured she was full of shit about us making the patients nervous. I've been here every fucking day since Tabitha was snatched. Like Scout said, that first day or two we got some extra female attention, but after that, we became part of the furniture. I haven't observed anyone reacting to our presence. Well, apart from Mia, but we already know she's in on things."

"Ms. Mason, care to tell us what's going on or would you rather Keys tell you what we know?"

Scout's voice was calm. Too calm, but this twit didn't know him well enough to know how much trouble she was in. With her chin still held high, she stayed silent.

"Volt's been calling you," he said. "Every day."

I lunged forward, toward her, which had her squealing and backing away. I'd kill the stupid bitch for helping Volt get to Tabitha. Scout stepped in front of me and physically held me back. Which was only effective because I respected him too much to knock him on his ass.

"Ms. Mason," he said. "I would suggest you explain yourself and quickly. I won't be able to hold my brother back for long."

"It's not my fault! I had no choice! He... He's got a video of me. I don't even remember it, but he's got a video. If I didn't help him, he'd release it on the internet. I tried to get around it. I didn't turn off the right alarms that night so the cops would be alerted to Tabitha being taken. That made him mad. If I don't get all of you out of here by tonight, he's going to grab me, and make more videos."

With a shake of his head, Scout looked to the carpet for a moment. "For fuck's sake."

I shook free of Scout and paced away. Lilith was another fucking victim. Volt needed to be put down, and fast. He was as bad, if not worse, than Godfrey. It made sense the fuckers had found each other. Like attracted like.

Scout rubbed a hand over his head as he sighed. "You've read the notes from Mirabelle's and Tabitha's files. You know what he did to you to get that video. It's a drug called Oblivion. It wipes your memory while it makes you sex-crazed. We'll be taking Tabitha and Todd with us today. You'll never see or hear from us again. He should back off once we're gone. If he doesn't, go to the cops with it. If they don't do anything for you, let me know and we'll see what we can do. Volt is fixated on Tabitha, has been for a good long time. I suspect he'll follow her, not you."

With a nod, she reached to grab a tissue from the box on her desk, that she used to dry her eyes and wipe her nose.

Scout ran a hand through his hair. "You should have come to me the first time he contacted you. We would have dealt with it sooner. Was he behind Mirabelle's kidnapping too?"

She shook her head. "No, he only ever wanted to know about Tabitha."

I shoved forward past Scout. "And what about Mia? How's she connected to all this?"

She took a step back again as Scout grabbed my arm. "Leave her be. She's another victim in this shit."

She might be a victim, but she could have told us about the blackmail, warned us when they were coming for Tabitha.

"I can't discuss her with you. HIPAA laws. But I assure you, she's mentally unwell and needs to be here."

I tensed, contemplating beating the information out of her, but Scout tightened his grip.

"Relax, Arrow. Keys will dig up the info. We'll find the connection." He focused on Lilith. "Get all the paperwork sorted. As soon as I can get a cage up here, we're moving them out. You won't know where they're going so don't even fucking ask."

Tabitha

My head was spinning from how fast things were changing. I wasn't prepared for it all, hadn't had time to process what needed to happen. Volt was coming for me. He'd infiltrated Lone Oaks and it was no longer safe.

The club would protect us. To do that, we had to move.

Arrow and others from the club brought a van, packed Todd and me in it, and drove us around in what felt like circles before we left Houston and came back to Bridgewater.

Now I was in my own room on the top level of the Charon MC's clubhouse and Todd was next door, also in his own room. They were much like a hotel room, basic furniture and fixtures, with a small en-suite bathroom attached. I didn't mind the fact they were small. They were clean and the shower had hot water. More than I'd had at some of the places I'd lived in growing up.

I shook my hands out as I paced the room. I couldn't work out how the club had thought this was safer than Lone Oaks. Volt could get in anywhere. Find people to bribe or blackmail wherever I went. Or send in someone he already had under his thumb. Like he had with Mia at Lone Oaks.

I'd never be safe again.

My breathing increased and I started moving faster, trying to outrun my thoughts.

A knock on the door had me looking for a shadow to hide in but I couldn't get enough air in my lungs, couldn't breathe. I shook my head, trying to clear the jumble but it did no good.

"Tabitha, look at me."

I glanced up to see Veronica had come in.

She moved to stand in front of me. "Breathe with me for a minute, okay? Deep breath in… and out."

I followed along with her, matching my breathing to hers.

"That's it. Just breathe. That's all we need to do for now. Just. Breathe."

My lungs stopped burning, but my mind was still spinning.

"Okay, keep the deep breathing going while we work on relaxing your muscles. Let's start with your fingers. I want you to focus on your right hand. On relaxing your fingers so they're not clenched into a fist."

Closing my eyes, I internally focused on my hand. On one finger at a time, relaxing each one, getting them to straighten out. Veronica stayed with me, talking me through relaxing every muscle until I was finally feeling level again. With a final deep breath, I blinked open my eyes and looked at her.

"Thank you."

She smiled sweetly. "I understand all about panic attacks and hitting triggers. I still hit them sometimes, but it does get better. Do you know what set this one off?"

"I think it was just everything changing so fast."

She nodded. "Getting overwhelmed will do it. Come and sit on the bed, and I'll let you know what the plans are for going forward. Help you process what's going on."

I followed her lead and sat on the edge of the bed.

"As you know, Lone Oaks isn't safe for you anymore. The men got word that Volt was going to try something tonight so they got you and Todd out of there before that could happen. I'm going to be staying here while you're here so I'm close by for you, okay? Blade and I will be in the room across the hall so if you need anything at all, you come knock on that door and I'll be with you."

I nodded, feeling calmer knowing she was staying so close. "Thank you."

"The club is going to set up a new rehab center here in Bridgewater. They're getting Dr. Stringer to come and run it, but that'll take time. She needs to give notice and we need to find a building and get it fitted out. So, until then, you and Todd will stay here. The clubhouse is the safest place for you. No one gets in here without everyone knowing about it. Keys has cameras everywhere and while you and your brother are staying here, he has a team watching those cameras twenty-four/seven. You are safe here. As far as Volt is concerned, Arrow's been working on tracking down every detail of his existence for a while now. They'll find him and take care of him. In a permanent manner. Is there anything else you want to know?"

I shook my head. "Not at the moment."

Veronica nodded. "I'm not a trained counselor or anything like that, but like you I'm a survivor. My uncle groomed me almost from birth. I was thirteen the first time he raped me. I was thirty-two when the club took him out and I was finally able to break free. I got away from him a couple of times between those two dates, but he always managed to find me. So yeah, I get where you're at, what you're going through, and I'm here for you. The whole club is. Anything you need, just ask and if we can give it to you, it's yours. Okay?"

I nodded again. Emotions clogged my throat, making it hard to talk.

"How…" I wasn't sure I should even ask her. I didn't want to bring back her hell with my questions.

She reached out and took my hand between hers. "How'd I get past it? One day at a time. And if a day is too big, it's one hour, one minute, one second. Every moment you're moving forward, surviving another breath, living another minute. It gets easier. After being held captive for so long, the world is too big. It's loud and scary and too much to handle, but we'll help you ease back into it and before you know it, you'll be walking around on your own, smiling at the beauty of the day with no fear it's all going to end any moment." She gave me a smirk. "That part gets a lot easier once you know the one who hurt you is dead and buried and can't come back."

I wiped the tears from my eyes with my free hand and smiled at her. "I hope so. I don't want to be trapped anymore."

She squeezed my hand. "We'll help you fly free again. Just you wait. There's a whole world out there for you to explore and conquer."

I chewed my lower lip. The whole world seemed way too big for me at the moment, but maybe with Veronica and the club at my back, I could be brave and risk exploring a tiny piece of it. If I could just get Volt to leave me alone, I might even be able to enjoy it.

Chapter 15

Arrow

Sitting at the bar in the main room of the clubhouse, I threw back a shot before tapping the glass on the counter for the prospect standing behind it to get me another one.

"What's got you wanting to forget?"

I shook my head as Blade came to stand beside me. He got the prospect to pour two whiskeys and he picked them up. "C'mon, brother. Let's go sit down and have a chat."

I didn't want to talk. I wanted to get blind drunk so maybe I could fucking sleep without thinking about the dark haired woman who haunted me day and night. In the two weeks since she'd been living here at the clubhouse, I hadn't been able to get myself to leave.

It'd been over a month since I'd been out to my place down on the coast, which was the longest it had ever been between visits. I needed the space and fresh air to keep myself centered, but I hadn't been able to leave her. Until we found Volt and took him out, she wasn't safe.

"Still no news on where that fucker is hiding?"

I shook my head as I sat and took the drink Blade handed me. "Nope, fucker's found a hole somewhere to crawl into that we can't locate. We've been checking out everywhere we learned that he's even looked at in the past, but so far nothing. He's a sneaky bastard."

Blade nodded and sipped his whiskey before he spoke. "These assholes are smart. They gotta be to get away with all they do, but we'll nail him. He'll slip up at some point. No one can be careful forever."

"Well, I'd wish he'd hurry the fuck up so we can catch him. End this shit."

"What you planning to do once we get him and she's free?"

I stared into the whiskey as I swirled it around the glass. That was the million-dollar question.

"She ain't ready for me, for any man. She needs to learn to stand on her own, without a crutch she'll get sick of."

"Is that what happened with you and a past woman? Because let me tell you, that's not how things are with most couples. I ain't Veronica's crutch, but she sure as fuck knows she can lean on me when she needs to."

I took a gulp of the whiskey, enjoying the burn. "My folks. Mother was an addict. But in the end, me and my dad weren't enough to keep her clean, so she left to be with her first love—her drugs. He was never the same. Six months later, he took off and my grandparents got stuck raising me." I shook my head. "I ain't doing that shit. Swore I'd stay single forever. I got the club. They're enough family for me."

Blade nodded. "I never would have thought I'd end up living the wedded bliss life, but it's not so bad. Veronica is my other half, couldn't imagine my life without her now. I'm thinking your folks may have simply not been the right fit. They tried to make it work but they weren't right for each other. When you find the one that matches up with you, that shit ain't gonna break. And Arrow, I shouldn't need to tell you that Tabitha ain't no addict. She's fucking strong, brother. Hell, she escaped her kidnappers despite being drugged up and barefoot. And scared out of her mind. That is not a woman who's going to fall into relying on any kind of drug."

"I really don't want to get into this shit."

He laughed darkly. "Yeah. Well, Mr. I-Tell-It-Like-It-Is, payback is a bitch. Although, I will say, watching you be all quiet and surly around her is funny as hell considering you're never stuck for words with anyone else." He set his glass down and leaned forward, making sure he had my full attention. "That woman up there? She's a fucking keeper. She's the type of woman who will give her man the whole world. She'll always be there for you. She's seen suffering, she's been hurt, but she's still here, still breathing, fighting to rise above that. What man wouldn't want a woman that strong by his side?"

I took another mouthful of whiskey instead of answering him. He knew the fucking answer.

He leaned forward, waiting for me to look him in the eye before he continued. "Honestly? Being with a woman who's survived what she has, has some landmines you gotta watch out for. Hell, Veronica still hits a trigger every now and then, but we deal with it and move on. Trick is to not dwell on it, not let her dwell on it. Veronica hates when she has a panic attack, especially if anyone sees her having it. So, when Tabitha has them—and she will—you help her get through it and then forget it happened. That's the way forward. Don't be her fucking crutch she leans on, be the hand that pulls her up into the light. Lead her forward. She'll get stronger and more confident as time goes on. You being at her back will help her do it faster, but if you want to be an ass and not claim her, that's your choice. Someone else will see her for the gem she is and step up."

The thought of someone else, some other man, "stepping up" with Tabitha had me gripping the glass so tightly it shattered.

"Fuck!"

Blade shook his head as he grunted. "Yeah, like I said, you need to quit bullshitting yourself, brother. Every damn man here can see you're feeling her. And she's watching you damn closely. I'm not telling you she's ready for you to pin her to a wall and fuck her hard, but I'm guessing she wouldn't be opposed to a kiss or two. Hold her fucking hand, pretend you're teenagers and take it slow with her. Romance her, because I can guarantee that woman has never had any man give her anything nice in the past."

A prospect came over and handed me a towel and I wrapped it around my bleeding hand as he cleaned up the mess I'd made.

"Blade, enough, brother."

I got up and weaved my way over to the stairs. Dammit, I was drunker than I realized. Fucking shots did it every time. I eventually made it up the stairs and pounded down the hallway toward my room, which was right next to hers. I bet Scout did that shit on purpose too. Whole fucking club was a bunch of gossipy matchmakers. As I reached for the door handle with my left hand, a gasp behind me had me turning to see Tabitha in the shadows of the hallway just outside her door.

"Hey, *engill*. You thinkin' of going downstairs for a bit?"

I'd go back down if she was. No way could I let her loose alone with all the single brothers down there. Nope. Especially now the club whores were all over the place, not just in their room. She was way too sweet and pretty to be left alone down there at this time of night.

She shook her head and crept closer. "You hurt yourself."

I couldn't tear my gaze from her as she slipped up closer to me. She was so fucking pretty with all the brown hair and her big chocolate-colored eyes.

"Just a cut. Nothing to worry about."

She frowned. "It's dripping."

I looked down to my hand to see it was in fact dripping blood onto the floor.

"Aw, fuckin' hell."

By the time I rewrapped the towel, and looked back up, she'd disappeared into the shadows. With a sigh, I opened my door and stumbled in, but before I could kick it shut, it swung further open. Veronica came in with a first aid kit and Tabitha behind her. My gaze got stuck on her. It was like she was a magnet, drawing me in.

"I'm fine," I said. "Just bleeding like hell 'cause I'm drunk as fuck."

Veronica smirked and rolled her eyes. "Go into the bathroom and wash it under some cold water. Let's see if you need stitches or not."

Tabitha

Arrow was indeed drunk as fuck, but that didn't answer why his hand was cut up and bleeding. As Veronica patched him up—thankfully he didn't need any stitches—Blade came up the stairs and stopped at Arrow's doorway, spotting me even though I was in the shadows.

"My woman in there with him?"

I nodded. "She's fixing his hand."

"Good. Fucking idiot. You okay? All that blood didn't trigger anything?"

I gave him a smile. Like most of the club, Blade was always sweet around me. He could be a little too conscious of what might be a trigger for me, but I didn't mind. It was a nice change to be surrounded by caring men rather than abusive ones.

"Blood doesn't bother me," I said. "Just worried how badly he hurt himself."

"It shouldn't be too bad. It's bleeding like a bitch because of all the alcohol in his system. Thinned his blood. He gripped a glass too tight and it shattered. He forgets how strong he is when he's this tanked."

"He's talking fine. He can't be too drunk."

He smirked. "Darlin', Arrow's the size of a fucking mountain and used to drinking. It takes a hell of a lot before it'll affect his speech. However, it apparently doesn't take all that much to affect his ability to think. Probably best to leave him be tonight."

With that, he headed down the hallway to his room, leaving the door open. A few minutes later, Veronica declared Arrow was all patched up before she went the same way as her man.

Arrow came out of the bathroom and I couldn't tear my gaze from him. He'd taken off his cut and shirt while he'd been in the bathroom. His biceps had to be the size of my thighs. His arms, shoulders, and chest were covered in ink. His well-defined abs were ink-free and the light played over the ridges as he moved over to the door that he eased closed, like he didn't want to make any noise.

Had he forgotten I was in the room? How could I get out without him noticing me? Maybe I should wait for him to fall asleep then sneak out? Or should I say something?

I closed my eyes and started taking deep breaths like Veronica had shown me.

I could do this. I was an adult and Arrow was safe. I was safe here. He wouldn't hurt me, no matter how drunk he was. In the last two weeks, no one here had been even slightly threatening. And this was Arrow. My rescuer.

I opened my eyes, and my lungs froze when my gaze met his. He was standing there, his uninjured hand still on the door as he stared at me.

I licked my lips. "I should go."

Releasing the door, he turned toward me, giving me a full-frontal view of his bare chest. My fingers itched with my curiosity of how he would feel.

"You don't have to. You're welcome in my room, *engill.*"

Before tonight, he hadn't called me that since I'd moved in here. It had rather felt like he'd been avoiding me. I forced my gaze up from his body to his ice-blue eyes. Maybe while he was drunk, he'd be willing to answer my questions.

"Why did you stop calling me that? Before tonight, you haven't called me anything other than Tabitha since I came here."

With a sigh and a shake of his head, he shifted his injured hand up so his arm rested on the wall over my head. He was leaning in close enough that his warmth and scent surrounded me. Leather, pine, whiskey, antiseptic… aside from those last two, it was his familiar scent and it calmed me even as my blood pumped faster at his close proximity.

Seemingly as mesmerized as I was, he lifted his uninjured hand until it was near my face. I didn't look away from his eyes as he brushed his rough knuckles down my cheek.

"So soft…"

Tingles followed in the wake of his touch as he continued to brush his knuckles then his fingertips over my face. My lips parted as I panted to get more air in, and his thumb was there, rubbing over my lower lip.

"My grandpa used to call my grandma *engill*, before she passed away." He shook his head. "I stopped with the pet names because I was trying to put some distance between us."

He stopped talking, just staring at his thumb that was still stroking over my lower lip.

"Not that it helped," he said. "Seems I'm incapable."

"Incapable?"

It was difficult to focus on speaking with him touching me like he was. His hands were callused and rough but his touch was so gentle, it was completely different from anything I'd experienced before.

"Of leaving you the fuck alone. I should. You should leave."

A well of bravery I didn't know I had, surged up and made me bold. "I don't want to leave. I like being this close to you. I like how you make me feel. Are you going to kiss me?"

His expression turned to one of longing before he shook his head. "I shouldn't."

"Why not? We're both adults. I can barely remember the last time I was kissed."

He frowned and slid his hand down to my neck. His palm was so large when he wrapped it around the front of my throat, his hand covered more than half of my neck.

"They didn't…"

He stalled out but I knew what he wanted to ask. His focus on my neck had me thinking he was remembering the shock collar Godfrey had put there. That heavy metal ring was so different from the warm strength in Arrow's flesh. I would have thought anything on my neck would trigger a memory but Arrow's palm wasn't tight. He wasn't restricting my breathing at all. It felt like a protective claim.

"They didn't want to kiss me, Arrow. I haven't been kissed since high school. Are you going to change that? Or are you going to let my past end the night for us both? Send me back to my cold bed with nothing but the reminder of how he stole everything from me."

He growled, an animalistic sound that had my heart pounding even faster. He licked his lips and I turned my face up, encouraging him to take what he wanted from me.

"Please, Arrow. Show me what it's like to be cared for. Just once.

Chapter 16

Arrow

Fuck, this woman slayed me. Just once? I feared once I started, I'd never stop. She was my addiction. Blade had thought I was worried that Tabitha would become an addict, but that wasn't it; it was that I was like my father. I'd be addicted to her. I'd love her to the exclusion of all else.

Her throat moved against my palm as she swallowed and I inhaled deeply, filling my lungs with her sweet scent.

Just once.

One taste.

I could do this. I was not my father.

Lowering, I rubbed my lips against hers, and with a whimper, she rested her palms against my pecs. The second she curled her fingers into my flesh, my need for her roared to the front of my mind and pushed everything else aside. Releasing her neck, I shifted to cup her jaw, holding her still for me to take possession of her mouth with mine.

I swiped my tongue over the seam of her lips, and she opened for me. With a growl, I thrust my tongue in, finding hers and coaxing her to move with me. She was hesitant, clearly unsure what to do but she soon relaxed under me, moving her lips against mine, dancing her tongue against me.

When I pulled back to catch my breath, she stared up at me with dazed eyes. She looked more drunk than me, which considering all that alcohol I'd consumed earlier had burned off the moment I touched her, made sense.

Her left hand stayed on my pec but her right crept up over my chest. She slowly, tentatively stroked my beard. I hunched down and wrapped an arm around her waist to lift her up. With a squeak, she wrapped her legs around my waist and her arms around my neck as I moved to sit on the side of my bed. Settling her on my lap, I smiled at her shocked expression.

"Explore away, Tabitha. Whatever you want."

She smiled shyly at me as her gaze shifted over my face and chest. It was a nice boost to my ego to have such a beautiful woman be this overwhelmed with how I looked with no shirt on. I slipped my uninjured hand up under the back of her shirt so I could stroke the soft skin on her lower back. She tensed before she relaxed again and put her palms back on my chest.

I watched her as she traced over my tattoos, her intense concentration so fucking adorable I wanted to kiss her again. I wanted to strip her bare and love on her till the sun rose.

I stopped that train of thought before it could take hold. She wasn't ready for that, no matter how much my cock throbbed with my need to get inside of her. She went back to stroking my beard, before she moved a little higher and traced my lips. When she made a second pass over my lower lip, I opened my mouth to suck in a breath. She was killing me with her gentle exploration, but I vowed I'd let her do her thing. I wanted her comfortable with me. With all of me. And it wasn't like I wasn't enjoying this little session either. Having a sexy as hell woman sitting on my lap running her hands over me like I was some rare and treasured sculpture was no hardship.

"Your beard is soft." She moved to run her fingers through my hair that I'd left loose tonight. "So's your hair."

"Gotta take care of it right if you want long hair, *engill*. Same with a beard."

She smiled a little and went back to running her nails through my beard. I kept it trimmed fairly short. It wasn't anywhere near as long as Scout's or some of the other brothers, but it was thick and full and her hands in it felt great.

"I had to figure out how to cut my own hair. It's long because I was never brave enough to try to cut it shorter."

Pulling my hand from her lower spine, I moved it up the back of her neck until my fingers were buried in her long brown locks.

"It looks good. Soft and healthy. You did a good job. You wanna get it cut short? I can take you to the hairdressers and you can get whatever you want done to it."

She smiled and a spark hit her eyes. "Maybe I could dye it?"

Fuck, but she was so damn innocent and sweet. Even with everything she'd been through, she was almost childlike in moments like this when simple things like choosing to dye her hair made her light up.

"Darlin', it's your hair. You can do whatever you want with it. Dye it blue with yellow streaks if you want. It's all up to you."

She giggled just like I'd hoped she would. "Not sure about the yellow streaks, but blue might be a nice change. Although, I don't have any money."

I rubbed my fingers against her scalp, massaging her a little and loving how she nearly purred.

"I got you covered, and you'll have your own money soon enough. Club'll make sure you get a cut from Godfrey's estate. He stole your savings. That's not right and we'll make sure you get at least that back."

"You're too good to be true."

Her whispered words shot through my heart. I needed to stop the hero worship shit she was pulling, no matter how much I fucking loved it.

"I ain't no hero, Tabitha. I'm just a man."

She gave my beard a small tug and leaned in to lightly kiss me. "You'll always be my hero, Arrow."

Before I could respond to her whispered words, she was kissing me again and I lost my fucking head at the feel of her lips against mine. I wrapped my arms around her and pulled her in tighter against me. My cock throbbed against my jeans and I pulled her ass in so her torso was pressed up against my hard length.

With a gasp, she broke the kiss.

"Arrow…"

"I'm here, *engill*. Right here with you. Fuck, that feels good."

I ground in against her again as I took her lips once more. Damn, I was right. One taste was never going to be enough. Never.

She wrapped her arms around my neck, burying her hands in my hair, running her nails over the shaved undercut as she groaned into the kiss. Needing more, I gripped the bottom of her shirt and lifted it up, breaking the kiss to get it over her head, easily ignoring the bite of pain in my hand from the cuts as I bared her skin to me. Her bra was black satin with absolutely no fuss to it, but she looked like a goddess in it.

Returning to her lips, I reached behind and flipped the catch open. I nuzzled my face in against her throat, kissing the tender skin there as I tugged the bra down her arms and out of the way. Pulling back a little, I glanced down and nearly came in my fucking jeans. Her nipples were small and tight with her arousal and I couldn't resist the sweet pink tips. With an arm around her back, I guided her up on her knees so I could nuzzle my way down her chest to them. My beard would tickle her skin and make her more sensitive.

Leaving one arm around her back, I cupped her breast in my other palm, lifting it up so I could get my mouth on it. The first lick had her tightening her grip in my hair and whimpering. I swirled my tongue around the tight little tip, and she arched her hips in against me.

Fuck, I wished we were naked, that I could pull her down and impale her on my cock.

Tabitha

Sensations bombarded me, making my head spin, but in a good way. I forced my eyes to stay open, and kept my hands in his long hair. I didn't want the past to rise up and ruin this.

Arrow was so different from any of Godfrey's men, and if I could stay focused on him, I should be fine. With a groan, he switched his mouth to my other breast, his hand staying where it was, tweaking and kneading the nipple he'd just had in his hot mouth. As he sucked on the other one, my body began to coil tighter. Arousal burned through me and I whimpered again when he gently bit down.

"Arrow…"

I wriggled my hips against him, wanting more. With a growl, he stood in a rush, turned, and laid me out on his bed. The gleam in his eyes had my lips parting so I could pant. He wanted me; he was desperate for me. This huge Viking god of a man wanted me this much. I gulped as he reached forward to undo my jeans.

The moment he had them undone, he gripped either side and tugged.

And my world flipped. I wasn't in the room with Arrow anymore. I was back in Godfrey's office that first time, pinned up against the door with Phil holding me in place for Godfrey.

"No! Stop, get off me! Help!"

"Aw, fuck. No."

I scrambled off the other side of the mattress, hitting the floor in a heap.

"Cut it all off. Her uniform is going to be changing anyway. No more pants or underwear for our little toy. We'll need easy access whenever we want it."

"Tabitha! Stop, you'll hurt yourself!"

I shook my head. I wasn't Tabitha, not anymore.

"You are my very own Martha. You will run around busying yourself doing anything I ask. That includes bending over so I can fuck you, or getting on your knees to suck my cock. Or any of my men. You are to do anything you're asked. Your new accessory is not just for decoration. It's a shock collar. You disobey, you'll get a shock. We'll be moving you to the new house today and once there we'll set the collar so you'll get a shock if you leave the house. You are to be seen but not heard. If you're good, you'll stay as my silent housekeeper and fuck toy. If you misbehave you'll be trained just like little Nina is being trained down the hall and put up for sale. Do you understand?"

Whimpering, I clawed at my neck, trying to get the collar off. A shadow came over me and with a cry, I tried to crawl away. "No, please…"

"You got something we can drug her with? We need to calm her down before she fucking hurts herself."

No, not that horrible drug. The things it made me do. A shudder ran through me and I shook my head.

"I'll be good," I said, whimpering. "I promise I'll do whatever you want, just don't dose me up. Not Oblivion. Anything but that…"

"Aw, fuck."

"Jacqueline left me a few doses in case this happened. You're going to need to hold her steady for me so I can deliver it. But wait till I get back."

That was a woman's voice. I shook my head and pressed my fists into my temples. Nothing made sense!

"C'mon, Tabitha. Come back to me, *engill*. Don't do this."

I didn't do anything! I never did anything wrong, but it didn't change what they'd do to me. Nothing ever made any difference. I cried out when I was lifted from the floor. I tried to push away but he was so strong. No matter how much I thrashed, he held tight.

"Let me go! I don't want this! I've never wanted it! Someone, help me!"

Why was I calling out for help? No one here would help me. They'd only help him. Help Godfrey abuse and hurt me.

"Veronica, hurry the fuck up. This is too much."

"Remember she's not lashing out at you, Arrow. It's her memories she's fighting."

A growl vibrated the chest I was up against and I pressed my hand against the colored skin. Ink. Tattoos. Godfrey and his men didn't have tattoos, not like this. Not huge ones that covered their chests.

"Well, I'm the one who fucking triggered this shit. What's that tell you?"

I inhaled deeply and smelled familiar leather and pine. I buried my face in against him just as a sharp pain hit my arm.

I recoiled away. "Ow! Get away from me! Don't touch me."

He didn't let go and as my mind slowed, I snuggled in against his warmth. Someone set a blanket over me. Suddenly, the strong arms holding me didn't feel like a threat but like protection and with a sigh, I burrowed into the embrace. As I drifted off, I couldn't help but wonder if I'd ever be able to be intimate with a man again without hitting a trigger and losing my mind.

Chapter 17

Tabitha

For the next two days, I hid from everyone except Todd. I was so mortified I'd fractured like that. I'd forced Arrow to pin me down so Veronica could drug me.

"You can't hide in here forever, sis."

I'd been curled up on a chair, with my knees tucked up under my chin, beside his window but straightened, putting my feet back on the floor as I looked over at where Todd sat on the edge of his bed lacing up his shoes. The move to the clubhouse had done wonders for Todd. He'd started venturing downstairs and hanging out with a couple of the younger guys who'd been taking him to the gym with them to help him get his physical strength back.

He was getting better. Progress was slow, but it was happening. Without me. I was still stuck.

"You don't know what happened," I said.

He rolled his eyes as he stood.

"You had a flashback. They're gonna happen, Tabitha. Especially when you're with a man." He winced, and turned to make his bed. "I don't think I'll ever be comfortable enough to have a lover, but the fact you even tried is a big step forward."

I only knew a little of what was done to Todd, but I could read between the lines. I knew he'd been raped. And Bess had told me how Godfrey had he said Todd was gay, and that he'd been handed over to him by a cousin to "cure", which was a lie so the whole thing was probably complete fiction. But I'd been meaning to talk to Todd about it. If he was gay, I wanted him to know I didn't care. That it didn't matter.

"You've thought about having a lover? In the future? You know, I'd support whoever you chose—"

He spun on me, stopping me mid-sentence.

"Seriously? You think I'm gay? You believe that bullshit Godfrey spun? My own fucking sister doesn't know me well enough to know that was nothing but one of his mind fucks?"

The fury radiating off Todd had me freezing. I had no idea how to combat his rage. I'd never seen Todd angry like this. My heartbeat skipped and started hammering and I felt sweat bead on my forehead. What would he do to me? I didn't mean to make him angry.

"Fuck, Tabitha. Don't look at me like that. I'd *never* hurt you. Never. But I'm not fucking gay. Never was. I hate that everyone thinks I am what he forced me to be."

He stormed out, leaving me alone to force down my fear and memories on my own. I stayed there in the seat, staring out the window for a long time.

Is that what everyone thought of me, too? What Godfrey made me? He'd made me into a whore and housekeeper. What was I here at the clubhouse? The little mouse that Needles called me? I'd done nothing but hide in the shadows and watch the others. Except for when I'd been with Arrow two nights ago. My skin tingled in memory of his touch, but he'd left me again. The next morning he'd been gone. Veronica told me he'd headed out to his place out of town for a few days.

I'd sent him running. Forced him to leave his family because I was here.

I couldn't be inside anymore. I rushed to my room and put on my sneakers before I jogged down the stairs and toward the front door. No one stopped me as I broke free into the light of day.

I paused at the bottom of the steps and tilted my head up to the sun before the sound of a bike had me looking toward it. But it wasn't Arrow's motorcycle. I had no idea who'd just arrived, but I didn't care. I headed toward the gates with my heart in my throat.

They'd said I wasn't being held captive, that I could leave whenever I wanted. I hadn't tested it till now, but today I needed to feel free. Even if it was for just a few minutes.

Biting my lip, I walked out of the gate, forcing my feet to keep going when what I really wanted to do was run back inside and hide. When no one stopped me, I giggled. I was doing it. I was free! Walking out in the world. On my own.

Free.

The clubhouse was on the edge of town and there weren't many houses around it. I made it to the end of the street and stalled out. I looked both ways at the two direction choices but didn't know which way to go. An engine revved to my right and I looked up to see a car in the distance coming for me.

Fear shot through me and I realized how stupid I'd been. Volt was still out here; still had his men watching. I spun and started running back toward the clubhouse. I'd gone further than I thought. The engine was louder as it got closer and knowing I wasn't going to make it, I veered off the road and hid behind a large tree. With my heart pounding in my ears, I could only just make out the sound of the car as it flew past without slowing down.

It wasn't after me.

I was just being paranoid. I blew out the breath I'd been holding and keeping my eyes closed, took several deep breaths, focusing on each one until my heart rate calmed down.

Arrow

After the clusterfuck with Tabitha, I'd taken off. A few days at my place down the coast was just what I needed to clear my head and get grounded. Although, as I rode back to the clubhouse, I still had no fucking clue what to do about her. She was under my skin and affected me like no woman ever had before, but I couldn't be with her if I caused her to flashback like she had. Watching her suffer like that had torn my heart from my chest.

Pulling into the yard, I headed inside just in time to see Scout guide Todd over the back corner of the main room. Todd had been coming downstairs more and more the longer he stayed here, hanging out with a couple of the younger prospects. I'd been thinking he'd be looking to prospect in himself soon, but maybe not with the way Scout was growling at him.

I went over to see what was going on.

Scout had his hands on his hips and his head tilted down, sure signs he was not a happy man. "What did you say to send her flying out that door? I won't ask again."

I stopped a few feet from them. "Who'd you send running, Todd?"

Scout cursed and ran his hand over his head. He used to wear a bandana that he constantly adjusted, but his old lady had gotten him to ditch the thing so now he messed with his hair when he was on edge.

"Arrow, stay calm. She's being watched. She's not a fucking prisoner, but I want to know why she took off."

Tabitha had left. My heart sank. I wanted to go look for her and drag her back here where I knew she was safe, but I forced myself to stay where I was. If Scout said she was being watched, she was.

Scout growled to Todd. "Talk to us, boy."

"She told me it was okay to be gay. I'm not fucking gay. That was a lie Godfrey told everyone as part of the mindfuck portion of my torture. But that's what everyone believes! No one's said a thing to me about it—"

Scout shook his head and ran his hand through his hair. "Stop right there, kid. First up, none us believe a damn thing Godfrey had to say. The reason no one's talked to you about it is because no one gives a fuck. Ain't nothing wrong with being gay. We've had gay brothers in the club, got at least one or two currently."

I turned to Scout. That was news to me. Who the fuck was gay? Not that it mattered, but damn, now I was curious.

Scout chuckled before he continued. "Yeah, we all got our secrets. See? Even Arrow didn't know and he's an officer. No one's said anything because that's your private biz. If you wanna share, go for it, but no one here will pressure you to spill your secrets. So, what happened with your sister was you lashed out and stormed out, then after she dwelled on it for a bit, she went charging out the front door like the world was on fire and she was the only one with a bucket of water?"

I scrubbed a hand over my face while Todd mumbled his response.

"Yeah, somethin' like that."

Before we could continue, the front door opened and I turned to see Tabitha slip back inside, looking pale. She pressed herself against the wall next to the door.

I went to go to her, but Scout grabbed my arm.

"Todd has something to say to her first, don't you, kid? Make shit right with that woman. She's your family, your blood. You don't let shit like this sit and rot between you. Nothing good will come from it."

Todd nodded and with his head down made his way over to Tabitha.

Scout folded his arms across his chest and kept his gaze on Todd. "He's a good kid. And he's come a long way, but damn, he needs to work on that quick temper of his."

"Guessing he's always been impulsive. He did run off to look for his sister. Have you heard anything from his foster family?"

Scout nodded. "I got in contact with 'em a while back. They have another two foster kids they're taking care of now. They've asked me to keep them updated on how he's going but they can't take him back in. Not that he'd want to return to Louisiana when his sister is here."

A shard of fear sliced through me.

"Do you think she wants to move back?"

Scout rolled his eyes. "She ain't leaving you, dumbass. Fuck, of all the brothers, I didn't expect you to be the one who couldn't see what was right in fucking front of him. Try taking her out of here. Clearly, she's feeling cooped up and wants to see the world, but she still ain't ready to do it on her own. Take her for a ride down to Marie's Cafe or something."

He walked away before I could answer, leaving me to stew on my thoughts while Todd spoke with Tabitha. I waited for him to finish so I could go over and do my own groveling. I shouldn't have left without telling her where I'd gone. Had she been worried?

Fuck.

When she reached up to tuck her hair behind her ear, I remembered our conversation from the other night. Before it all went to hell. She wanted to dye her hair.

Pulling out my phone, I rang Cindy. She'd know where I could take Tabitha to get what she wanted. Hopefully that'd be enough to earn her forgiveness for leaving her. Again.

Chapter 18

Tabitha

As I sat into the cushioned hairdresser's chair, I glanced out the front window again. Making sure my Viking hadn't left me.

Cindy giggling had me looking back to her. She'd accompanied me on this outing and I was enjoying her company. She was so enthusiastic about everything. "He's still there, honey. Trust me, Arrow ain't going nowhere. Now, before Deirdre comes over, what do you want to do? Something totally out there, or just a trim and tidy up?"

I gave Cindy a frown. "Do you normally get this excited when other people get their hair cut?"

She laughed and gave my shoulder a friendly tap. "Hell no. Arrow mentioned you hadn't had a hair cut in forever and I knew Deirdre would fit you in for me. So—" She paused to wriggle her eyebrows. "You gonna go totally wild or what?"

Deirdre laughed as she pulled up another chair and sat next to me. "How about we look at some ideas?"

She pulled up an app on her tablet and searched for current hair trends.

"Let me know if you see something you like, and we'll look for more things like that. Did you want to keep it long, or go shorter?"

I twirled a lock of my hair around my finger. It hung down to nearly my elbow and I wanted it gone. It was too much of a reminder of what my life had been for so long.

"Short. I want something different."

"Okay." She tapped a few times at the screen and it filled with images of all sorts of styles in a myriad of colors.

"That one!" I pointed at one of the pictures. "I want that. The color and everything."

Deirdre tapped the screen to enlarge the image, while Cindy clapped her hands together. "This is going to be epic! Bring on the makeover!"

I couldn't help but smile at Cindy's enthusiasm as I kept looking at the image.

"That'll look great on you. Sweet little stacked bob with a side part and a little extra length in the front. So, you want the same color? A steel gray-blue at the roots and a brighter blue on the tips?"

I nodded.

"Great! I'll just go get the colors sorted and we'll get rolling."

While Deirdre went to mix up the colors, I looked from the image up to Cindy.

"Do you really think it'll look okay?"

She grinned at me. "Oh, yeah. You're going to rock that color and cut. And once it's all done, I'm taking you to Retro Funk for some new clothes. Gotta do this makeover properly."

I shook my head. "Oh no, that's not necessary. I don't have any money! I already feel bad enough about Arrow paying for this."

Cindy leaned in and wrapped her arm around my shoulders, giving me a quick hug.

"Honey, you're family. We've got it covered."

Before I could argue with her anymore, Deirdre came back rolling a cart with pots filled with creams on the top.

"Right, let's cut some of this off first, then we'll color and finish cutting, okay?"

I shrugged. "You're the expert."

She chuckled and set about her work. I watched in the mirror as she shortened the length to just above my shoulders. With each piece of hair that hit the floor I felt lighter. Godfrey had liked my hair long. He'd liked to wrap it around his hand to control my movements. This new cut would be so short up the back that no one would be able to use it against me.

I'd never admit to anyone that was the reason I wanted to go so short, but it was the truth. I would not be a victim again and cutting off my hair was the first step.

A few hours later I sat, shocked mute, staring at myself in the mirror.

Cindy didn't have the same issue and started gushing to Deirdre. "You've worked your magic again, Deirdre. She looks fucking epic. Arrow's gonna trip over his tongue when he sees you."

Grinning, I tilted my head around to see all the sides of my new hair. I'd really done it. I'd cut off all my hair. I looked so different, I wondered if Volt would even recognize me anymore. Wouldn't that be a dream come true? Volt not knowing who I was.

Cindy made me hide behind a display case while she brought Arrow in and got him to pay the bill.

"Okay, close your eyes," she said to him. "Don't look at me like that, just do it. Trust me, it'll be worth it."

Arrow grunted, but he sounded amused. "You're a pain in the ass, Cindy. Nitro really should be doing something about that, considering what you're into."

Cindy laughed. "Oh, he tries, trust me. But at the end of the day, he loves that I'm a brat. Now, quit stalling. Close your eyes."

"Fine."

I was nervous about what Arrow would think of my new look. Cindy hadn't taken me to her store yet for new clothes, but my hair was so different. What if he hated it? Wouldn't look at me anymore?

I couldn't believe I actually wanted a man to look at me now. For so long, I'd wanted nothing more than to not be seen by anyone.

"C'mon, Tabitha. Reveal time!" Cindy called. "Wish I could have gotten you dressed up too, but we can't go anywhere without an escort, so we'll have to make do."

She tugged me out of my hiding spot and pulled me to

the front of the store. Chewing my lip, I dragged my feet, unsure what Arrow would think or say. He stood there looking proud and strong, his Charon MC cut rested over his large frame as though he'd been born to wear it. Today he'd braided his long blond hair, so he looked extra Viking-like.

He was so damn gorgeous. How did I think for even a moment he would notice me?

Cindy stood behind me, her hands on my shoulders and she leaned in to whisper near my ear.

"Don't worry, he's gonna love it. I promise. If for some strange reason, he doesn't, I'll kick his ass for you."

The mental image of Cindy trying to take on Arrow made me chuckle.

Arrow

Women were fucking nuts. Making me close my damn eyes in the middle of the fucking salon like a sap. I'd be telling Nitro about this one and he could dish out some punishment. He was her Dom, after all. He really should have her better in hand than this.

Not that I understood the whole BDSM thing.

"Okay, Arrow, now you can look."

With a sigh at how stupid I felt doing this shit, I blinked open my eyes. As soon as I saw Tabitha, I couldn't look away. Fucking hell, she'd done it. She'd gotten all that beautiful long hair cut off and dyed what remained blue.

Well, it looked more gray at the top and blue on the bottom, but whatever, it was totally different and looked amazing.

"Arrow, say something," Cindy said. "You know, before you freak her out that you hate it."

"Fucking love it."

Before I could stop myself, I strode up to her and after placing my palms on either side of her neck, slid them up through the short hair, finger combed the longer lengths before dropping my hands away.

"Gorgeous, *engill*. You like it?"

She nodded, looking up at me wide-eyed, as though I'd shocked her.

Cindy began guiding Tabitha forward. "We're not done. Wanna take her to Retro Funk next for some new threads."

I shook my head but didn't look away from Tabitha.

"Sorry, Cindy, not today. You took longer in here than planned. Tabitha's got an appointment she needs to keep."

She winced and looked down, but with a finger under her chin, I lifted her face back up.

"Don't you be embarrassed or ashamed, Tabitha. You've been through hell and came out the other fucking side. Be proud you're smart enough to know you're gonna need some help to adjust to life now that the hell part is over."

Tears glistened in her eyes and a spear of pain sliced my heart right open for her. She was so fucking strong but couldn't see it. Leaning in, I pressed a kiss to her forehead, not giving a fuck who saw.

"C'mon, Tabitha. Let's get you to Dr. Stringer. You can go shopping with Cindy another day, I promise."

With a nod, she let me lead her outside to the cage I'd been forced to take because I couldn't fit both her and Cindy on my bike. I still hadn't managed to get her on the back of my Harley, but I vowed I would soon. Scout was right. Along with Blade. And Nitro.

Fuck, all those meddling matchmakers were right. Tabitha was mine. At least, I wanted her to be. I just needed to focus on not letting her become my addiction. If I could just hold back enough that I still had other interests outside of her, I could do it. The other married men in the club did. They had their old ladies and still did shit with the club, still had their brothers' backs and did other stuff.

We really were short on time, so I had to drop Tabitha off at the house we'd set Dr. Stringer up in for now before taking Cindy to her shop. I walked my girl in and handed her off to the prospect guarding the front of the building. There was another on the rear entrance. Keys was still working on getting all the cameras and shit wired into the system, but that would be up and running in the next couple of days. Tracking Volt had been our main priority for the moment and Keys was still training those of us who'd joined Athena Security, so a lot still fell to him to handle.

As Tabitha slipped inside, I stopped beside Gypsy, a

newer prospect, who was walking the line of the front of the property. "Everything good here?"

"Yep. Quiet morning. Nothing unusual going on."

I nodded. "Good. I need to go drop Cindy off, then I'll be back. Keep a close eye on Tabitha until I get back. Understand?"

He gave me a nod and stood a little straighter. He was a good kid. A little lost and looking for somewhere to call home, but most prospects were.

I turned and rushed back to the cage, wanting to get Cindy dropped off as quickly as possible so I could return. I hated leaving Tabitha.

I took a turn a little fast and with a laugh Cindy grabbed the oh-shit handle.

"Need to install those five-point racing harnesses in club cars with how you boys drive. Damn, Arrow. You still mad I made you close your eyes earlier? Wanna get rid of me or something?"

I scoffed and slowed down for the next corner. "That shit was annoying but nothing worth holding a grudge over. Don't take it personally. I just don't like leaving her alone."

Cindy reached over and patted my thigh. "She's not alone. Two prospects and the doc are with her. Keys got the doc's panic button sorted out, right?"

"No clue. He's still wiring up the cameras and shit. Was planning to finish it off tonight, I think. We would have held off starting up but after the past couple days, Jacqueline wanted to see Tabitha today."

Cindy nodded. "Fair enough. Need to get her processing that shit before it drags her too far down. She was really scared you wouldn't like her new hair. She didn't say anything, but I had to basically drag her out from behind that display for you to see her. She likes you, Arrow."

Seriously? Not only were my brothers on my case, now the women were gonna join in, too?

"Cindy, she ain't ready. We proved that the other night. I can wait."

"Maybe *you* need a session with the doc. Talk to her about how to handle Tabitha's triggers. Blade and Veronica handle it okay."

Thankfully, we pulled up at Retro Funk before I had to come up with an answer for her. With a sigh, she got out and I waited until she was inside before I took off toward the new clinic. Without Cindy to bitch about my cornering, I got back in record time, but I knew it hadn't been fast enough as soon as I pulled up. Gypsy was nowhere in sight and there was a sense of dread hanging around the house. I pulled my cell out as I got out and bolted toward the building.

Scout answered on the first ring. "Arrow, what's up?"

"Something's wrong at the clinic. I had to drop off Cindy. I just got back and Gypsy ain't on the front door like he was when I left. I'm going in now."

"I'll call in the troops. Be there soon."

Pocketing my phone, I slammed through the front door, praying Tabitha was okay.

Chapter 19

Tabitha

"Hello Tabitha, nice of you to finally grace us with your presence."

I skidded to a stop as I rushed through the door into Dr. Stringer's office. Since I was running late, I hadn't stopped to check, to make sure the area was safe. I mentally kicked my own ass for not taking those few moments as I stared at Mia standing behind a very pale, frightened Dr. Stringer with a knife to her throat. Just because I hadn't seen or heard from Volt since coming to Bridgewater didn't mean I was safe. So stupid.

"What do you want, Mia?" I asked, fighting down a shudder.

Dr. Stringer sat still at her desk, but her chest heaved with barely restrained panic.

Mia grinned, a glint in her eyes. "Well, what I want doesn't much matter, does it? For some reason, Volt wants you, so you he gets."

A sting in my neck was the first I was aware there was someone behind me, and as my vision went dark, I knew it was already too late to do a damn thing to help myself or Dr. Stringer.

I woke to a slap to the face.

"Ah, finally. You're gonna wake the fuck up. Lazy bitch."

With a groan, I tried to move but couldn't. Blinking my eyes clear, I found myself shackled to a wall in what appeared to be a basement of some sort. The walls were stone but it was hard to see much else. The only light came from a battery-operated lantern sitting on the floor right next to Mia.

"Where am I?"

"Oh, a little place just out of town," she said, as she ran her gaze around the room. "The Charons tried to burn it down a while ago, but they didn't do a very good job. Just think… you're in the same shackles that once held their precious president."

She landed a punch against my ribs and tears sprang at the jolt of pain. Whatever she'd drugged me with was still in my system, making things foggy. But this didn't seem right. Volt wanted to use me, not beat me. He'd never hit me. Not once.

"You're with Volt?"

She sneered at me and hit me again, this time on the opposite side. Pain radiated from both sides enough to steal my breath.

"I would be with Volt if it wasn't for you. What the fuck do you have that I don't, huh? What's so fucking special that he'll sacrifice everything just to get his hands on you?"

She gripped my jaw, digging her fingers into my cheeks until I was forced to open my mouth.

"Not like you got a tongue ring or anything special. Guess you must be real good at sucking then, huh? Or maybe it's your pussy that's so fucking magical. Maybe your ass."

A female moan came through the door and I jerked my head at the familiar sound. *Oh, no.* Shivers wracked my body and the chains rattled.

Mia laughed.

"Oh, yeah, the good doctor is getting some therapy. I swiped a few vials of Oblivion the last time I saw Volt. Dr. Stringer is keeping the men distracted so I can have some fun with you before the boss comes. A little bonus for them helping me capture you earlier."

Tears flowed as a wave of guilt crashed over me. It was my fault. Dr. Stringer, who'd done nothing but try to help me, was in the next room being gang-raped while high on Oblivion. All to provide a distraction.

"She's innocent," I said.

Mia backhanded me hard enough my head hit the wall, making my vision swim. "No one is truly innocent in this world. That bitch diagnosed me with all sorts of bullshit. Schizophrenia! Right. I'm not fucking crazy, and I don't need meds. What I need is you to die so Volt won't be obsessed anymore. But since he'd also never forgive me for killing you, I'll just make you so ugly he can't stand to look at you. You did half the job for me with that bullshit you pulled with your hair. Blue? Really?"

I could barely focus on her as she lifted a blade. Another shiver rolled through me as she gripped my jaw again and brought the shiny metal in closer.

"Hold still now, hate to slip and take out an eye or something important."

I whimpered as the blade flashed in front of my left eye. She wouldn't really cut out my eye, would she? Surely, she wasn't that nuts?

The blade lowered as Mia laughed but my relief was short-lived when the tip dug into my flesh under my nose. Pain flared in a line down over my lips and chin. She held my jaw firm to stop me from pulling away while she made a second slash before she released me to step back with a manic laugh.

Clenching my jaw to keep it shut, I tried to get enough air in through my nose to breathe through the pain. She'd cut a fucking X over my mouth. Agony took over. I couldn't think, couldn't hear anything past the pounding pain. Every spare ounce of focus I had went into keeping my mouth closed and not screaming out. I knew if I did, I'd probably choke on all the blood. The smell of it was bad enough, making bile churn in my stomach.

"Fuck, that's making one hell of a mess," she said, sneering at me. "You better not bleed out on me and fucking die. He'll forgive me for a fit of jealousy, but not murder."

I barely felt her cut my shirt and bra off, but when the tip of the knife traced over my nipple, she had my full attention again. Fuck.

"I was going to cut off your nipples but now I'm thinking that would have you leaking way too much blood…hmmm."

She slashed up the inside top curve of my left breast and the trail of fire had me screaming. I couldn't stop it. As I'd anticipated, my mouth filled with blood and I spat it free, desperate not to choke on it as I panted through the newest agony.

Mia shrieked. "You bitch! Don't spit blood at me, you dirty whore. Let's see how he likes you after I really *fuck* you up."

She started to tug at my jeans and my whole body shook. The chains rattled and my thoughts went fuzzy. I was losing too much blood. So much blood. An image of Arrow filled my mind, and I closed my eyes to focus more fully on it. I wanted him to be my last thought.

Arrow

Keys' office was getting crowded with all the club officers jammed in here waiting on Keys to do his thing. Finally, the location on Tabitha's tracker came in, but I couldn't believe it.

"For real? We destroyed that place."

Keys shook his head at my outburst. "Not completely. It was a rush job. We destroyed the lab, made sure that all burned, but we didn't have time to level the place.

Guess we should have gone back and finished the job."

It'd been a year since Scout had been taken by Volt's cousin and held hostage. Fucker also got hold of Marie and her foster sister, Sarah. We'd gone to get them back, but it'd been too late for Sarah. Marie and Scout were now raising her daughter, Ariel, who'd been conceived thanks to that fucking drug Oblivion.

"Got no time to spare on this one. We need Volt alive. You hear me, Arrow? Need him to be able to fucking talk. Ending Oblivion is the end-game we need to aim for."

I snarled at Scout. "Rescuing Tabitha is the fucking end game."

"No, it fucking isn't. That's our first priority, to rescue both Tabitha and Jacqueline, but if we don't get to the bottom of where this fucking drug is being made, there's going to be a lot more Tabithas in the future. I'm not saying she should sacrifice her life for the greater good or anything. I'm saying let's do this smart and get the girl, and have the bad guy breathing at the end, yeah?"

I looked him in the eye. "I'll try, but I can't promise anything."

He held my gaze. "Fair enough. Let's ride."

I'd never mounted up so fast in my life and was first out of the gate. I didn't give a fuck about the rest of the club in that moment. I promised Tabitha I'd keep her safe and I'd failed. She'd been snatched and we'd lost our fucking doctor in the process, too.

When I pulled up at the building we'd attempted to burn down a year ago, memories flooded back to me. Finding Scout chained to that wall was burned into my mind, an image I'll never forget. The end of the building that had housed a lab was nothing but a burned-out shell. The whole place looked abandoned, aside from the sole van sitting to the side.

Assuming they'd have the women in the basement where Scout, Marie, and Sarah had been, I jogged toward the burned-out section to gain entrance, pulling my weapon as I slipped into the unburned section.

The roar of bikes pulling up didn't quite drown out the moans and grunts coming from down the hallway. My rage grew with every step closer I got. Lifting my gun as I turned the next corner, I came upon four men all fucking Jacqueline.

Beyond grateful that not only had I spent so much time at the gun range, but that I was in the habit of carrying my tactical 9mm, I didn't waste time in taking aim and pulling the trigger. I nailed two before any of them realized I was in the room and killed the last two before they could do anything about it.

I moved toward Jacqueline, who was clearly jacked up on Oblivion and unaware of what was going on around her.

Nitro and Machete came in. Nitro briefly rested a palm on my shoulder. "We got this."

I nodded and left the room, knowing they'd get her out to Keys, Blade, and Veronica in the tank and dealt with.

With my weapon up, I kept going, aiming for the basement rooms. I sensed the others behind me, having my back, but didn't bother to see who it was. I trusted all my club brothers to have my six.

When I finally made it into the room, it took a few moments to process what I was seeing.

"Get the fuck away from her, or I'll shoot," I said. "Already killed your crew, so it's no sweat to send you to hell, too."

Volt didn't move from his position. He was leaning over Tabitha's body on the floor, his back to me. "Do that, and you'll kill us both. You got a medic with you?"

I glanced over to Mia, who lay crumpled against the wall, her neck at an angle that made it obvious she was dead.

"Of course, we do. What the fuck's going on here?"

"Mia sliced her up. She's losing too much blood. I'm putting pressure on the wounds, but you came storming in here before I could do anything else." He looked over his shoulder at me. "What's it gonna be? Kill us both or get her some help?"

Scout brushed past me before he skirted around the room toward Mia.

"Wish I never had to see this particular room again." He checked Mia for a pulse, but we all knew she was dead. He then moved over to Tabitha's other side, so he was facing me. With a frown, he ran his gaze over her. It was doing my head in that I couldn't see where she'd been slashed up.

"Where's she hurt, prez?"

"Face and chest."

With sharp movements, he planted his foot square in Volt's chest and kicked him away from Tabitha before he dropped to his knees and took over holding pressure to her wounds. Mac grabbed Volt and zip-tied his wrists before he could recover from being winded from Scout's kick. I was stuck staring at my girl. There was blood everywhere. So much fucking blood.

"Scout…"

I couldn't even get the question out, but how could she be alive?

"She's breathing, brother. Head wounds bleed like a bitch. You know that. Keep your head level so we can get her outta here and into the tank. She needs the hospital."

In a trance, I watched Mac drag Volt out before I snapped out of it. After putting my gun away, I knelt down to press a kiss to her temple.

"You fight, *engill*. Don't you dare give up on me."

I got busy helping Scout and my brothers get my woman out of this hell hole and to hospital.

Chapter 20

Tabitha

Through the haze of pain I was in, a beeping echoed around my mind. Voices filtered through.

"You need to take care of yourself, brother. How you gonna protect her? Fall on her?"

"I don't matter. I ain't leaving her side, Nitro."

"What happened wasn't your fault, Arrow."

"How do you figure that? I promised her I'd keep her protected and then I wasn't there when she needed me and now look at her. That fucking bitch sliced her up."

The words floated around my mind, not really making much sense, but I knew it was Arrow talking closest to me. And he was mad, his voice laced with fury. I needed to make that better for him, needed to soothe his beast. I wasn't worth getting upset over.

I tried to open my eyes, but my lids were too heavy to move. I swallowed and tried to speak, tried to open my mouth, but agony flared across my face and a sob welled up.

"Ah, fuck, Tabitha, don't try to talk, darlin'. Your lips

are damaged." His calloused fingers slid into my hand and I squeezed, as my eyes stung with emotion. He was real. Arrow was here. "You squeeze my hand once for yes, twice for no, okay?"

I squeezed once.

"Good girl. Do you know where you are?"

One squeeze.

"You're in hospital. You're safe. We caught Volt."

Memories flashed behind my closed eyes almost faster than I could follow. Mia had men help her take me and Dr. Stringer. She'd cut me up. Dr. Stringer was given Oblivion and given to her men.

Oh, my God! What had happened to her? Was she okay? I couldn't ask that with squeezes for yes and no.

Arrow's voice sounded from beside me. "Go get the doctor. She's getting agitated about something."

Footsteps sounded, leaving the room, but Arrow was still holding my hand so it must have been Nitro who went to get the doctor. I needed to open my eyes.

I swallowed again, ignoring the metallic taste in the back of my throat, focusing on my eyes. *Open. Open, dammit.*

The first crack I managed had light overwhelming my vision and I shut them with a wince.

"I'll turn the lights off. I'm not leaving the room."

He released my hand and I felt cold and alone. No! I needed him back. I fisted the bed sheet, trying to focus on my breathing. On anything other than the absence of Arrow.

"Okay, *engill*, try again. Open your eyes. Let me see you're really back with me."

The sheet was tugged from my grip and he put my hand between both of his. Lifting my hand, he pressed kisses to my fingertips.

With a deep breath, I focused again and this time when I opened my eyes, the room was duller. After several blinks, I could make out that I was indeed in a hospital room and my Viking warrior was sitting in a seat beside my bed. The man had dark smudges under his eyes and his shoulders were slumped as though he was long overdue some sleep. He was still holding my hand up with my fingertips against his mouth. I shifted so I could stroke the softness of his lips. Lips that had kissed me. Lips…

Mia had cut my lips. My eyes went wide, and I lifted my other hand to my mouth. Arrow reached out and grabbed my wrist before I made contact and I glared over at him.

"You have stitches. The cuts were deep. I don't think it's a good idea to touch them yet. It's only been a few hours. They've barely started healing."

A doctor walked in. "Try several hours, but yes, it's best to not disturb the stitches especially this early on. You can suck on some ice, if you want. That'll help reduce any swelling and ease some of the pain."

I gave him a nod. Couldn't touch my face. Not supposed to talk. How the hell was I going to communicate? I looked around the room until I saw a mirror through the bathroom door. I looked to Arrow, then to the mirror, back and forth until he followed my gaze.

"You want to see? I'm not sure that's a good idea."

I wrapped my hand around his fingers and squeezed once, hard.

He looked up at the doctor. "Have you got a mirror she can use? Guess she's determined to see the damage."

"I'll get a nurse to find one while I check her over now that she's woken up. I'll get her to grab that ice for you, too."

He briefly left the room before returning and doing all the usual crap doctors did. I kept my gaze on Arrow's face the entire time, barely tracking what the doctor was doing. Arrow looked so worn out. The lines of worry etched on his face made my heart ache. I wanted to tell him it wasn't his fault. Mia would have gotten to me eventually. And the longer it took, the crazier she would have become.

When I heard someone else come in, I tried to look around the doctor to see who it was. I wanted that mirror. And the ice. It would hopefully help wash the metallic taste of blood out of my mouth and throat. The doctor finished doing his thing and turned to reveal it was Veronica who'd come in with a mirror and a small cup.

"Excellent," the doctor said, stepping back. "Veronica will help you with the ice and with seeing your injuries. Please remember, they're fresh and will heal. They won't look like they do now forever. Now, I best get onto my next patient. Your club just about has a wing to itself at the moment."

That drew my focus from the mirror onto the others. Suddenly, I didn't care about what I looked like but instead wanted to know how everyone else was. Dr. Stringer had been raped, given Oblivion. I had no idea what had happened to the men guarding the clinic.

I swallowed and looked to Arrow, who was closest.

"The others?" I tried to speak without moving my lips and the pain wasn't too bad.

Veronica moved to sit on the other side of me as the doctor left.

"Jacqueline—Dr. Stringer—should be waking up soon. She was sedated so she could sleep through Oblivion's effects. We'll need to wait for her to wake up to see how she is. Physically, she'll heal quickly, but due to the Oblivion, we just don't know what her mindset will be. The prospects who were on guard duty were knocked out with a hard strike to the head. They've both been in overnight due to having concussions. Thankfully, like most men, they have hard heads and they're otherwise fine. Well, they're feeling guilty as hell they didn't do their jobs, but physically they'll just have a headache for a few days."

I nodded and closed my eyes. Poor Jacqueline, all she'd wanted to do was help people. She'd never hurt anyone. Mia had hated her because she'd tried to help her. It wasn't fair.

I cleared my throat and looked to Arrow. "Mia?"

"She's dead."

He paused and looked to the door, then to Veronica.

She crossed her arms over her chest, clearly not leaving any time soon. "My lips are sealed. I want to know, too."

"Our women aren't supposed to know club business. You know that."

"We also like to sleep at night, so spill. We know how to keep a damn secret."

He frowned at Veronica but shook his head. "Fine. Because I've been here all night, I don't know much. Information is still being gathered, so to speak. But it looks as though Volt came in when Mia was doing her thing and he killed her then got you down and tried to stop the bleeding."

"Her men?"

I was trying to limit how much I talked, and Arrow kept glaring at me whenever I spoke, but I wanted to know what had happened, so he could just get over it.

"All dead."

The ice in his gaze and the set of his jaw told me that was all the info I'd get on that subject and honestly, as long as they were dead, I didn't care. I turned back to Veronica and lifted my free hand for the mirror. It was easier to move now. My body just needed some time to come back online when I first woke up.

"Are you sure you want to see right now?" she asked.

I nodded as I stayed focused on the mirror she still held facing away from me.

"Well, okay then. Like the doctor said, it won't always look this bad. It needs to heal. We had a plastic surgeon do the suturing so hopefully once it's all healed up, you'll barely see the scars."

Tears stung my eyes, but I forced them down. I needed to see. See how Mia had scarred me. Made me ugly just like she said she would.

Veronica glanced at Arrow before, with a sigh, she put the edge of the mirror against my palm, allowing me to take hold of it. Pulling my other hand from Arrow's grip, I used both hands to move the mirror up so I could see my face. My reflection shook as I trembled, but I could still clearly see the cuts Mia had made and the neat black stitches that held them closed. I had an uneven cross over my mouth. That bitch had sliced the right to left cut all the way from just under my nose down to my chin. The left to right was shorter, starting close to the other side of my nose but only going down to just below my lip. My vision blurred and I blinked it clear, not caring that tears were running down my cheeks.

No matter how well this healed, I'd always have a big X over my mouth. I'd be disfigured for life.

Shifting my grip on the mirror, I freed one hand so I could grab the front of my hospital gown and tug it down. Adjusting the angle of the mirror I took in the slash over the top curve of my breast. It would easily show if I wore a V-neck t-shirt.

Forgetting I had company, I shoved at the sheets, needing to see what she'd done lower, after I'd passed out. Arrow grabbed my wrists while Veronica took the mirror.

"Stop, Tabitha," he said. "There's no more. You still had your jeans on when I found you."

I looked to him, my tears blurring his face. "She was going to fuck me up with the knife."

My lips tugged as I spoke, but the bite of pain was nothing compared to the remembered agony of the knife slicing me open.

"She didn't. You weren't raped, *engill*, I promise, that didn't happen."

Needing him to ground me, to make it all better, I pulled free of his grip and reached for him, wrapping my fists in the fabric of his shirt he wore under his cut. He cupped my face in his palms, resting his forehead against mine. I breathed in his scent with every breath I managed and slowly my mind settled. Before long, my lids grew heavy and Arrow guided me back against the mattress as I drifted off.

Arrow

I ran my knuckles down Tabitha's cheek as Veronica fussed with her drip.

"You slipped her something, didn't you?" I asked.

"Sure did. There's no reason for her to get herself so worked up. She needs rest to heal, not to get so upset she's at risk of popping stitches."

I nodded but didn't say anything else as she slipped out of the room, leaving us alone. I stared at Tabitha's face, now lax with sleep. Life had not been fair to her. So much pain and loss.

"She still sleeping?"

I glanced up to see Todd coming through the door with Scout on his heels.

"Uh, she woke up a little while ago, but they just gave her a sedative. She got upset after seeing the wounds."

Scout didn't come in far. "I'm going to check on the others. Back in a few."

Todd had his arms wrapped around his middle as he came over and sat on the other side of his sister. His gaze didn't leave Tabitha's mouth.

"She didn't deserve this. She hasn't deserved a damn thing that's ever happened to her, but the world keeps shitting on her anyway."

I gave him a nod. "Was just thinking the same thing."

He was silent and I didn't try to fill it. They'd both been through a lot, more than what I knew about.

"How much older is she?"

He frowned but didn't take his gaze off Tabitha. "Twelve years. She was sixteen years old when Mom died giving birth to our sister. We lost her, too. She rolled with it, became my mom. She always made sure I was taken care of along with our stepfather. She lost her own father when she was a toddler, and mine skipped out before I was born. But Mikey did his best to be our dad. At least before Mom and the baby died, he did. Then he hit the drugs. Cocaine. Everything went to shit after that. Volt had his men come and rough Mikey up while she was at work. She got home just as they broke my arm. Child services took me away, and the next thing I knew, she'd run off and sent me a letter saying she had to go."

He shifted and picked up his sister's hand to hold, tracing her fingers with his own.

"Guess we weren't enough, you know? Like, I get he loved my mom and his baby and missed them, but surely the kids he already had were worth living for, weren't they?"

He looked to me and I felt cornered by his questions that hit way too close to home.

"I don't know, Todd. My situation growing up wasn't that different. It was my mother who couldn't stop with the drugs, then after she left, my father just gave up. Well, he spent six months looking for her, then he came home, packed me up, and took me to my grandparents and left. I know how it feels to grow up thinking you were never enough."

His gaze was piercing in its intensity and I had to force myself to sit still and not squirm under this kid's scrutiny.

"You know that's how Tabitha felt when you stopped coming to see her at Lone Oaks, right?"

Heat raced across my cheeks and I hoped the dim lighting hid the color from Todd.

"None of us are perfect, Todd. We all fuck up at some point or another."

With a shrug, he looked back to Tabitha. "Yeah, even

when we mean well, it can fuck things up. Like when I made shit worse by coming to look for her. I should have just left it alone. But no, I had to go trying to do what she's always done."

How on earth was this kid taking blame for what Godfrey had done to his sister?

"What's that?"

"She's always been there. You know, fixing shit. Making it better. I just wanted to help. Instead, I loaded more guilt on her and every time Godfrey got mad at me, he took it out on her."

Aw, fuck. I was no therapist, but I had to try to ease his pain. I couldn't let Todd carry his own load of guilt when he'd done nothing wrong.

"Godfrey was good with the mind fucks, Todd. You know that. From everything I've read about the man, he preferred young males. I'm fairly certain, once he got you, he wouldn't have spent much time with Tabitha. Did you talk to Dr. Stringer about how you're feeling?"

He shrugged and went back to playing with his sister's fingers. I guessed it was something he'd done as a child as he didn't seem to be aware he was doing it.

"Don't feel right talking about it."

"I can understand that, but she's got the training to help you get through it all. She won't judge you for anything that happened. No one in the Charon family will."

"Yeah, well, from what I overheard, she's gonna be busy dealing with her own shit for a while now."

I winced. "Not sure how that's gonna play out yet. We'll have to wait and see. If she does need some time off, we'll find another therapist to bring in. Maybe a male?"

He shuddered. "I think that would be worse. I could never admit to a man what happened to me. No way. It's too embarrassing."

I leaned forward, and Todd looked at me again.

"I need you to focus on what I'm saying, you hear me? Nothing that happened in Godfrey's fucked-up house of horrors was your fault. Nothing. Was what he did to Tabitha or Mirabelle their fault?"

He recoiled in the chair. "Fuck, no!"

"Exactly. The three of you were his victims. Hell, Todd, you were chained to a wall in a basement! There was nothing anyone could have done in that situation. You were a boy, trying to be a man in order to save his sister. Ain't one bit of shame in that. You did your best and paid a heavy fucking price for it. Stop beating yourself up, yeah? The three of you are all survivors, fighters. Don't lie down and let that fucker win now that he's rotting in hell. He doesn't deserve to have that level of control over anyone."

Scout strolled in with a look on his face that told me he'd heard most of our conversation.

"What you need, Todd, is a distraction. Something to fill the days. How about you start coming over to the bike shop with me? We'll see how you like pulling apart sleds and fixin' them. Sound good?"

Todd had stilled when Scout first started speaking but now his eyes were wide, and I could see he was thinking it over and liking the idea.

"I think that's a yes, prez. Although, maybe it should wait until after we get his sister back to the clubhouse and out of here."

Scout came over and patted Todd on the shoulder. "Done deal, if you want it, Todd. Just say the word."

Todd turned to look up at Scout. "Thank you."

"You're family, son. Anything you need, all you gotta do is ask."

Damn, but I loved being part of this club. I hoped Todd would go through with accepting Scout's offer. Learning a trade would be really good for his self-confidence. And if he made a home for himself here in Bridgewater, Tabitha would be more likely to want to stay, too.

Chapter 21

Arrow

It'd been three days since shit went down and even though I had Tabitha back at the clubhouse, I was still on edge. I didn't want to let her out of my sight, but I also wanted to have a piece of Volt before the fucker died.

"Arrow, go already. I've got her covered. And Blade's out in the hallway to make doubly sure. Poor Tabitha is long overdue some girl time. We're gonna paint our nails and talk about which of the male nurses is the hottest." Veronica shooed me. "Go. Be gone!"

I wasn't sure whether to growl or laugh at her. When I glanced over at Tabitha and noticed the sparkle in her eye, I grinned. So long as she was happy, it'd be fine.

"I'm not going far," I told Tabitha. "Let Blade know if you need me and I'll be back here in a flash."

She curled her legs under her, making herself comfortable on my bed. "I know, Arrow. Thank you. You need some time away from me, too. Go for a ride or something. You don't do well being cooped up."

Damn woman knew me too well already.

"Next time I get on my ride, you're gonna be behind me, *engill*."

I walked away before she could respond, loving the shocked look I'd put on her face. But by the time I reached the back stairwell, I was dead serious. Pushing through the hidden door, I headed down the stairs to the basement. Thanks to excellent soundproofing, I didn't hear anything until I passed through the cell door.

Taz tossed a pair of pliers onto the table that sat against the wall next to where Volt hung. "Hey, brother. You want a go?"

I nodded but kept my gaze zeroed in on Volt. He didn't look nearly as imposing now he was naked and hanging from chains. Taz had done a good job working him over. He always did, especially when it was someone who'd hurt women or kids. Volt's fucking drugs had caused harm to countless people.

"How careful do I need to be?"

Taz grabbed a rag to wipe blood off his hands. "Pretty sure I can get some more information outta him if I have more time, so try not to kill him. But if you do, it's not the end of the world. We got the drug lab locations outta him yesterday and Scout's taken a team down there to clean it out."

"So, he's confirmed it was the right location?"

"Sure did. The world's a brighter place already without anymore of that Oblivion shit in it. Well, I'm sure there are a few vials here and there that he's sold, but we're working on tracking them down and according to him, no one else has the formula. So yeah, try not to kill him, but it ain't gonna keep me up at night if you do."

He tossed the rag aside and headed for the door.

"I'm gonna go grab some grub while you have your turn. Back in a few. Oh, Arrow? Take your cut off before you start. Blood is a bitch to get out."

With a nod, I shrugged out of my club colors, hanging them on a hook near the door that was there for just that purpose. Then I shut the door and as it crashed shut, Volt's head came up and he squinted at me. I had no idea how much he could see through his swollen eyes.

"Surprised Taz didn't cut you up yet."

"Said that was someone else's job."

I grinned as I pulled a hair tie from my pocket and shoved my hair up in a knot at the back of my head so it was out of the way. "That'd be me, fucker. You ordered my woman be cut up?"

He shook his head. "Mia did that on her own. I never wanted Tabitha to be hurt. You found us. You know I killed her and saved Tabitha. Without me, she'd be dead."

I backhanded him hard enough the chains rattled. "Don't piss me off any more than I already am. If you hadn't wanted her, Mia wouldn't have gone after her in the first place. Hell, if you hadn't wanted her, she wouldn't have run and landed with Godfrey. Way I see it, every fucking thing that girl's been through is all on your shoulders."

He growled, like he had some game left, and I wanted

to laugh. Stupid bastard. I stood close, forcing him to look up to meet my eyes. I stood at six-four to his five-six. I was clearly the bigger, stronger man. Volt was a typical drug dealer. Looked about as threatening as a used car salesman. At least to me.

"She was always meant to be mine," he said. "My queen. I never would have hurt her. If she'd just come to me, she'd have been safe. I did what I had to with Godfrey because she ran."

Clenching my fist, I landed a heavy punch to his left kidney. If he lived long enough, he'd be pissing blood after that shot.

"You have no fucking clue what it means to have a queen, let alone how to treat one. You fed her your bullshit drugs so you could rape her easier. Wanted to take her in payment for her stepfather's drug debt. You never once took care of her, you fuck. But I will. She will be my fucking queen. Unlike you, I'll treat her right. While you rot in hell where you belong, she's gonna thrive. And you can die knowing that it's me taking care of all her needs, no fucking drugs required."

I stepped back as he tried to lunge at me, growling.

"She's mine! She was always meant to be mine. Not yours, not Godfrey's. Mine."

Taz slipped back in but stayed near the door.

"Sorry, Volt, but that's just straight up bullshit. She never wanted to be yours. Hell, she ran away from everything she knew. Nearly across the entirety of Texas to get away from you. What's that tell you? You had to drug her so you could pretend she wanted your scrawny ass."

He tugged at the chains again, trying to get to me. Yeah, Godfrey had one thing right. A good mind fuck did way more damage than physical pain. Maybe after I gave him a few other things to think about, Taz might be able to get even more names outta him. When he was due to die, I'd be the one to shove an arrow through his fucking heart. But that wouldn't happen today. He hadn't suffered nearly enough.

Tabitha

I couldn't hold in my curiosity any longer so I asked Veronica about Arrow. "You know what he's doing, don't you?"

Arrow had been gone for over an hour and as much as I'd enjoyed the girl time with Veronica, I missed him. Missed how I felt safe, protected when he was nearby.

"You don't want to know, trust me. He'll be back soon, I'm sure."

I sighed. "I'm not stupid. Naive, maybe, but not stupid. Volt's somewhere here, isn't he?"

"Club business ain't our business, honey. It's like the top rule in this place for us old ladies. What we don't know, we can't tell."

I rolled my eyes and reached to grab another ice chip from the cupful of them that Veronica had brought me earlier. I'd gotten to like sucking on them over the last few days.

"First, I'm not an old lady, whatever the hell that is. Second, who the hell would I tell?"

Veronica cocked her eyebrow at me as she painted my next toenail bright blue.

"When a biker claims a woman as his old lady, he's declaring to the club she's his one and only. For bikers, it's as solid as marriage. And we can all see it won't be long before Arrow claims you. As far as who? The cops, honey. If you get hauled in for questioning, you can't tell them what you don't know."

"Oh."

That was a lot of information to process. I focused on my fingernails that Veronica had finished. The blue polish had glitter in it that sparkled as I shifted my fingers. Not talking to the cops was an easy one. Even if I did know something, I'd pretend that I didn't. I'd never out the Charons. Not when they'd saved my life more than once.

"You really think Arrow feels that way?" I asked. "Every time it seems we're getting close, he up and vanishes."

Dipping the brush back in the bottle, she moved onto my final toenail. "He pulled that shit earlier, but from what Blade tells me, he's gotten over whatever it was that had him holding out. He refused to leave the hospital until you did, and did you notice the room you're in? It ain't the one you were in before. This is his room, honey.

You tell me what you think that means."

I just blinked at her. I mean, obviously I knew I wasn't in my room but Arrow's. I wasn't sure what it meant. I knew what I hoped it meant, but could I dare to believe?

"If I was sleeping in his room, where do you think he slept last night?"

She shrugged. "Where was he when you went to sleep?"

"In that chair."

"And when you woke up?"

I blew out a breath. "In that chair. He slept sitting up? All night?"

She gave me a small smile. "He did at the hospital. At a guess he didn't sleep much. Pretty sure I heard him prowling around a few times, no doubt making sure no one got anywhere near you."

"That's nuts."

He would have been so uncomfortable trying to sleep sitting on that wooden chair. I ran my gaze over the bed. Had he lain next to me to sleep? There was plenty of room on this big bed. But ultimately, Arrow was a gentleman, so I doubted he would have done that. Especially considering how things ended last time we were together in a bed.

"How do you feel about him?"

I looked up to Veronica, shocked. "What do you mean?"

After twisting the cap on the nail polish, she set it on the bedside table.

"Not all women like men to be as, well... blood thirsty

as Arrow has been lately. I mean, he went out early to go get you. Normally the club rides out together, with the tank bringing up the rear. But as soon as Arrow knew where you were, he took off. And he was pushing his bike hard to get to you. We didn't leave long after him, but when we arrived, he was already inside, shooting."

"Shooting?"

She winced. "I'm thinking this is one of those club business things we shouldn't talk about."

I glared at her. "Then how come you know? And you can't stop there. I want to know what happened while I was out."

"I know because I was in the tank and the guys talk. Normally, Donna goes, but she's got Mirabelle now and I was here already so they grabbed me. I'll tell you but you can't bring it up with anyone. You need to pretend like you don't know any of this shit, okay?"

I'd promise her anything to know what happened. "Sure, my lips are sealed. Now spill."

"Arrow stormed in and found four men in with Jacqueline. She was high as a kite on Oblivion. He shot all four of them. From what the guys were saying, Arrow is one hell of a shot. The others caught up with him then and took over with helping Jacqueline so he could keep moving to get to you. He found you out cold with Volt holding pressure over your wounds. Mia was dead."

I frowned. "I can't believe Volt saved me. He's been the monster in the shadows for so long, I just can't wrap my mind around him having any good in him at all."

Arrow strode through the door. "He doesn't. He sees you as his possession and was simply protecting his property." He scanned the room, along with Veronica and me before he started toward the bathroom. "He won't ever be waiting in the shadows for you again. You're safe now. I'm takin' a shower."

He shut the door and Veronica cursed under her breath.

"He was not happy. Fuck, I'm gonna get in the shit for telling you all that."

I reached out and grabbed her forearm. "I'll make sure he doesn't say anything to anyone. I forced you to tell me. In my shoes, he'd want to know. I'll make it right, Veronica. I promise."

She leaned over and wrapped an arm around my shoulders for a sideways hug. "Thanks, but don't worry too much about it. Scout'll just rant at me for a while about women staying outta club business. They won't hurt me or anything. Now, you relax and enjoy your new nails… and maybe your man. He could use some relaxation too, I think."

She winked at me and I chuckled.

"Yeah, well, the last time we tried that it didn't end so well."

She shrugged as she packed up all the nail stuff. "So, avoid the trigger you hit last time. I still hit them sometimes with Blade, but we take note of what it was and avoid it in the future. You'll be fine."

Chapter 22

Arrow

Fucking gossipy women. Veronica shouldn't have been telling Tabitha that shit. I was already running behind with trying to make her mine, last thing I needed was her out there imagining how I blew into that place and shot up a bunch of men.

I made fast work of washing my hair and scrubbing myself down, making sure I didn't have any blood anywhere on me. The faster I got back out there, the faster I could end their conversation. Who knew what ideas Veronica was putting in her head?

Would she even still be in my room when I came out? She hadn't said anything earlier about the fact I'd brought her back to my room, not hers.

I muttered to myself, "Just get back out there."

After roughly drying off my hair with a towel, I ran a brush through it before I wrapped the towel around my waist. I'd not thought to grab clean clothes on my way in so looked like she was getting me in a towel. Although, that could work in my favor. Last week when she'd seen me shirtless after I cut up my hand, she seemed to appreciate the view.

Shoving the bedroom door open, I was relieved to find that while Veronica had left, Tabitha was still sitting on the bed, her legs folded beneath her. She'd been looking at her nails but glanced up as I entered.

"Veronica shouldn't have told you that shit."

She winced and looked away. "Please don't be mad at her for it. I made her tell me."

With a shake of my head, I chuckled. "You made her, huh? Either way, she wasn't inside that building. She doesn't know what went down."

"Well, I didn't think *you'd* tell me if I asked, and she seemed pretty confident in her information. Why? What'd she get wrong?"

I shrugged a shoulder as I went to the closet and pulled out a pair of track pants. "Volt's a piece of shit."

"Well, yeah, but are you saying you didn't shoot the men that were raping Dr. Stringer?"

Squeezing my eyes shut, I pulled up my pants under the towel, trying to not flash Tabitha my ass in the process before I tossed the towel back into the bathroom.

I ran my fingers through my wet hair in frustration. "Why'd she even mention that?"

"I wanted to know."

I turned to look at her, still calmly sitting on my bed, looking so fucking fragile with her damaged lips.

"Why the fuck you want more reasons to hate me, babe?"

She flinched before returning to mess with her nails. I waited for her to say something, do something, but she didn't. Not until she wiped her eyes with her fingers and shifted to the edge of the bed.

I nearly missed Tabitha's whispered words as she headed to the door. "I'll just get out of your hair. Should have known it was all just in my head, no matter what Veronica said."

I moved to cut off her exit, blocking the way with my body. "What does that mean?"

Fuck it all, she was fucking crying. How had I made her cry?

"It means I could never hate you, Arrow. But you don't need to keep pushing me away. I get it. I'm too much trouble and not worth the effort. Too broken to bother with. Whatever you want to call it, I get it, so I'll just get out of your way and let you get back to your life."

Had she hit her head or something?

"How the hell did you come to that conclusion, Tabitha? I just spent the afternoon torturing a man for you. You think I do that all the time? You think I regularly walk into rooms and kill four men in under a minute? Think I rush outta this clubhouse ahead of my brothers, ahead of my president, to go rescue a woman?"

Her gaze had gone wide as I spoke, and when she stepped back, I followed her, guiding her until she was up against a wall.

"Only you, Tabitha. Only you have ever gotten that response outta me. From the second I found you standing in that fucking hallway with that damn shock collar around your neck, you've been all I can think about."

I paused to take a deep breath, trying to calm myself enough I didn't scare the hell out of her more than I already had.

"The reason I've been trying to resist this crazy connection we have isn't because you're broken or some shit. You're not, Tabitha. You're a little bruised at the moment, physically and mentally, but that'll pass. You'll heal from it. You're too strong to let fuckers like Godfrey and Volt keep you down for long. I've been resisting you because I'm scared *I* won't be enough for you."

I cupped her face and wiped her tears away with my thumbs.

"I wasn't enough for either of my parents. My mom was an addict. My dad got her clean and she was good for a while. They had me and she stayed clean. Until I hit school. Then she fell right back into old habits. I wasn't enough for her to stay clean. After she ran off, all Dad cared about was finding her, then after he did and realized she didn't give a fuck about anything other than the next fix even if it killed her, he took me to my grandparents and left, too. I swore I'd never risk myself like that again, never risk not being enough for someone I loved. Then you came along and fucked up all my plans."

I was saying too much. Fuck. With a sigh, I released her and headed over to my dresser and the bottle of Jack sitting there.

"I won't ever force you to stay where you don't wanna

be, Tabitha. If you want to go, you can. I refuse to be yet another man in your life who tries to clip your wings, *engill*."

I unscrewed the cap and took a swig from the bottle, closing my eyes as it burned all the way down. Lying to myself that it was the shock of the alcohol that had my eyes watering, not the fact my fucking heart was about to walk out my damn door.

Tabitha

It was fucked-up that Arrow admitting he was a little damaged too made me feel better. But it was a relief that I wasn't the only one of us who had issues. Silently, I padded over to where he had his back to me while he continued to drink whiskey straight from the bottle.

His hair was still damp and hung down past his shoulders, blocking some of the massive Charon MC logo tattoo that covered his back. I raised my hand and traced the feathered wing with my fingertip.

"You call me angel, but that word describes you better than me. You and your club are the ones who race to rescue those in trouble. The club had no clue Todd or I were in Godfrey's house but none of you hesitated to save us. Then once you saw us safely to Lone Oaks, you didn't wash your hands of us. I know the club paid for that place for all three of us. And you came to visit to check on me. Saved Mirabelle, then me when we were taken." I continued to trace the feathered wing that took up the left side of the tattoo. "You're the angel here. All I did was refuse to die."

He took another swig of the whiskey.

"One of the reasons they call me Arrow is because I tell people how it is. Always straight to the point with no bullshit. But you leave me speechless, Tabitha. I never know how to tell you any fucking thing. I ain't no angel. None of us are."

He set the bottle down, screwing the lid on slowly. Resting my left palm over that feathered wing, I lifted my right hand and began tracing the outline of the wing that looked more like a bat's, shifting his hair aside as I went. It was the darker, more sinister half.

"I see your dark side. I know you're not all pure and righteous, Arrow. No one is one-hundred percent good or bad. It's your dark side that had you pulling the trigger so quickly to save Dr. Stringer. Don't ever be ashamed that you have that side, and I hope you don't ever lose it."

He turned and I let my palms slide over his body until they rested against his pecs.

I looked up into his gaze. "I need your dark side, Arrow. That's the part of you that comes to my rescue, that won't let anyone get away with hurting me. It's the part of you that connects with the darkness inside me."

He winced as he lifted his hands to cup my face. "You're my light, Tabitha. There's no darkness in you. Even after everything you've gone through, you still shine bright."

I smiled as much as I could without pulling on the stitches in my lips. "I have darkness in me. I just don't have the skills to let it out to any effect. Might have to change that. Maybe you can take me to the range and teach me how to shoot like you can?"

He chuckled and shook his head a little. "Whatever you want, *engill*, it's yours."

His lips were so soft and had felt so good on mine. I swallowed down the ache that I couldn't pull him down to kiss me with my damaged face. His grip tightened and I looked up into his ice-blue irises.

"You want my kisses, *engill*?"

"Yeah." I lifted my hand to trace his lips with my finger before I dropped my hand back to his chest. "I love your kisses, but my mouth is messed up."

He hummed before he lowered toward me. Holding my face steady between his large palms, he pressed a soft kiss to the corner of my mouth. "I can still kiss you, just need to mix it up some."

He pulled back and I tried to follow him for another. I wanted more, dammit.

He chuckled. "We gotta take this slow, Tabitha. I don't want to hit any triggers again. That just about broke me, watching you suffer like that because of me."

I shook my head, tears pricking my eyes. "It wasn't your fault. It was Godfrey and his men who created the triggers, not you. I don't want to never have you touch me, make love to me, because of them. We can learn my triggers, avoid them. Last time it was you undoing my pants, so I'll just take them off myself in the future. Easy. Blade and Veronica do it. We can, too."

He squeezed his eyes closed and rested his forehead against mine. "You slay me, Tabitha. You really do. So strong. You're beautiful from the inside out, you know that?"

I pulled from his grip and touched my lip, the ends of the stitches pricking at my skin. The slashes would scar. I'd forever have an X over my mouth. That wasn't beautiful in any way.

Arrow wrapped his hand around my wrist and turned me back toward him.

"Scars don't mar your beauty—they're badges of honor, of survival. They're fucking real. No one gets out of life without at least a few of them. Take a closer look at me. All this ink hides the external scars. And trust me, I've got some wicked scars on the inside."

I ran my gaze over him, seeing the scars he spoke off, and the fresh scrapes on his knuckles. I lifted his hand.

"Is he dead?"

"Not yet. We're still getting information out of him, but it won't be long till we're done with him. Then we'll send him straight to hell."

I nodded, took a deep breath, and shifted my gaze from his knuckles back to his eyes.

"Can I be there when it happens?"

Chapter 23

Arrow

I stared at her for a few moments, not sure I'd heard her correctly.

"You want to be there? When Volt dies?"

She held up her chin, as though she expected me to refuse her when I'd just promised her she could have whatever she wanted.

"It won't be pretty, Tabitha. He's been worked over."

"Good. I don't want it to be pretty, Arrow. I want it to be messy and painful. I want to see that he paid a price for what he's done." She paused and cleared her throat. "And maybe if I see it with my own eyes, I won't dream about him. Godfrey still haunts me at night. I know he's dead and gone. I know you wouldn't lie to me about that, but I guess subconsciously it seems too good to be true, you know?"

I frowned. I didn't want her dreaming of me killing him. "I'll be delivering the final blow that'll kill him. Are you going to be okay with that?"

She actually rolled her eyes, which broke the tension

and had me smiling.

"If I didn't mind you shooting the men who helped Mia capture Dr. Stringer and me, what makes you think I'll mind you killing the man who started the downward spiral my life took all those years ago? If it wasn't for Volt, I never would have met Godfrey."

She clenched her fists and raised them into her line of sight. "I wish I was strong enough to do it. To end him."

I should let her. I should be the bigger man and step aside to let her make the final blow that killed him. But I wasn't sure I could. My inner caveman needed to take care of my woman, remove her enemies.

"We'll see."

That was the best I could do.

I shifted closer to her, wrapping my arm around her waist to bring her in against me, needing to hold her.

"You're gonna be the death of me, woman. For real."

I pressed a kiss to the top of her head before loosening my hold enough I could look down into her sweet face.

"Where did you sleep last night?" she asked.

I shook my head a little at the unexpected question. "In here. In the chair. Why?"

"Why didn't you sleep in your bed?"

"Because you were using it."

"It's a big bed, Arrow."

What was she angling for, here?

"I would never climb into a woman's bed without her permission. I'm not that sort of man."

"Yet you brought me to your room, not mine."

"Well, um…"

Of course, I'd brought her here to my room. She was mine. Therefore, she belonged in my room. But I wasn't sure she was ready for me to be claiming her like that.

Her hands slipped onto my waist and she smoothed them up until they rested on my pecs.

"Sleep with me tonight, Arrow. You will always have a place in any bed I'm in." She looked up at me, pleading in her gaze. "Please, Arrow, don't let my only sexual experiences be ones with those monsters. Show me what it's meant to be like. What it's like to be touched by a loving hand."

Motherfucker. Like I could resist that plea? Hell, I couldn't ever resist this woman, but especially not when she was blinking up at me with her soul showing in her eyes as she begged me to love her. Like she already wasn't the easiest woman to fall for.

I wanted to kiss her, to slam my lips over hers and possess her mouth before I moved on to take her body, but I couldn't. Those little black stitches holding together the slashes over her mouth were a stark reminder of what Tabitha's reality had been for so long. I made her a vow right then: she'd never know that level of pain again. With me, she'd never have anything but happiness and safety.

"We need to be careful of your stitches, *engill*. And you need to tell me if you start feeling uncomfortable. I need you to stop the moment you think we're heading toward a trigger, okay?"

"Yes, Arrow. *Please*."

With a growl, I leaned down and kissed the corner of her mouth, the best I could do for now. I pressed kisses over her cheek, along her jaw before I wrapped my arms around her waist and lifted her up so I could bury my face in against her soft neck. Fuck, she smelled like wildflowers in the springtime.

I moved us toward the bed, stopping when the backs of her legs hit the mattress. Lowering her down, I took a step back.

"Need you naked, *engill*. I wanna see all of you, touch all of you."

Her eyes dilated and she reached for her shirt, pulling it up and over her head. It took effort to not reach forward and help her, but that was what triggered her last time. Me tugging at her jeans. I wasn't risking making that mistake again.

Leaving her bra on, she reached for her pants. My gaze zeroed in on her fingers as they flipped open the button and lowered the zipper.

"You need to take yours off, too," she said.

"The second you get those jeans and underwear off, I'll be naked. I don't want to distract you before you get done."

She chuckled as I hoped she would and shoved her pants down over her legs. She'd put on a little weight since she'd gotten free and it was filling out her curves perfectly. I couldn't wait to get my hands and mouth on her.

Tabitha

The heat flaring in Arrow's eyes kept me going, removing all my clothes until I stood before him naked. For a full minute, he didn't move, just ran his gaze over my bared flesh. By the time he reached for the waistband of his track pants I was getting nervous he didn't like what he saw. Then he stripped off his pants and I was breathless for a minute myself.

All six feet four inches of him was beyond beautiful. From his long blond hair and blue eyes, down his muscular chest and abs, all the way down his tightly toned legs to his feet. And his cock was no exception. It was as large as the rest of him and stood tall and proud.

I'd never really looked at a man's dick before. I'd always tried to avoid them. But this was Arrow, and he was standing there as still as a statue as though I was a skittish colt that would bolt at the first flinch. I clenched and released my hands, not sure what to do. In the past, men had grabbed at me and forced things. I had no clue how this was meant to happen naturally.

"I don't know what you want me to do."

I just blurted it out. Nerves taking hold.

"What do *you* want to do?"

I carefully ran my tongue over the inside edge of my lip, avoiding the stitches and cuts. "I want to touch you, kiss your chest. Feel your warmth surround me."

He held out his arms. "I'm all yours. Touch away. Although, sadly, the kisses will have to wait a little while longer."

I nodded, forcing myself to not dwell on the reason for the lack of kisses, as I stepped up to press myself against his much larger frame. Being careful of the wound over the upper curve of my breast I cuddled in, sighing in bliss when he wrapped his arms around me, cocooning me within his strength. His erection lay between us, a thick rod against my tummy, but he didn't move to grind it against me or anything. He just held me as I relaxed against him, absorbing his warmth that fed my soul like nothing ever had before.

After a time, he pressed a kiss to the top of my head, then shifted to scoop me up in his arms.

"I can't give you too long, can I, or you'll get lost in that pretty head of yours. This is all about feeling, Tabitha. No need to over think anything, just do whatever feels right. Follow your heart, not your mind."

I rubbed my nose against his shoulder, the closest I could get to kissing him, and ran my fingers through his soft beard.

"That sounds perfect."

He lowered me down onto the mattress and stayed over me, his still-damp hair falling forward like a curtain. I reached up and took some of it between my fingers.

"Love how your hair feels, so soft."

With a smile, he dipped down and kissed the corner of

my mouth before he made his way over my cheek.

"Not as soft as your skin." He nipped my ear before nuzzling into my neck, pressing kisses as he moved down. His beard tickled my skin the entire time and by the time he got to my collarbone, I was squirming beneath him.

I wanted more.

My body arched up under him as he latched onto my nipple, laving it with his warm tongue.

"Arrow..."

As he continued to tease me, I ran my hands up his arms until I could bury my fingers into his thick hair, moving it out of the way so I could see what he was doing. With one last lick, he released my right breast and moved over to my left. He pressed a line of the softest kisses alongside the slice Mia had made before he moved down to tease my nipple like he had the other.

Without removing his mouth, he shifted to the side and slid his palm down my torso, over my belly button and further down. When he started to trace circles at the top line of my curls, I parted my legs, tilting my hips up, wanting him to go further down. Before he gave me what I needed, he lifted up and waited for me to lock my gaze with his. As soon as I looked into his ice-blue irises heated with arousal, he slipped his hand lower, his finger circling my clit before going further and finding my slick entrance.

"You feel so fucking perfect, *engill*. I can't wait to taste you here."

My eyes widened that he'd want to do that. I'd never had a man do that. I'd been forced to do it to plenty of men, but none had ever returned the action.

"Ah, sweetheart, you've never had a man go down on you?"

I shook my head, unable to form words as he grinned broadly.

"Oh, *engill*, I'm going to enjoy showing you how good this can be. Lay back and relax, love. Let me have some fun playing with your sexy body."

He pressed a quick kiss to the tip of my nose before he slid down, not stopping until he rested on his elbows just above my sex. He looked up at me and winked — making me giggle — before he lowered down and swiped his tongue up my slit. A gasp tore from my throat when he got to my clit.

Humming, he went back to do it again. I fisted my hands in the sheets and pressed my heels into the mattress, pushing myself up against his mouth to get more of the intense pleasure he was giving me.

"That's it, *engill*... so good. You taste so fucking good."

He shifted so his palms were under my ass and he tilted me up so he could get deeper into me with his tongue. Within seconds, my mind was spinning and I was panting to pull enough air into my lungs.

Chapter 24

Arrow

As shocked as I was that she'd never had someone go down on her, I was grateful for it. It meant I was unlikely to hit a trigger doing this. Which was perfect, because the moment I got her taste in my mouth, I was lost. I needed more. Needed to gorge myself on her sweet taste. Needed to make her come like this, so I could get more.

Lowering her back down to the bed, I removed my hands from her ass and ran my palms up the insides of her thighs, making her spread wider, opening her pussy up for me. Suckling her clit, I thrust two fingers deep inside and slid them in and out until she stiffened and moaned when I found her G-spot. Once I found it, I focused on hitting it with each stroke while I continued to tease her clit with my tongue and teeth.

Her body trembled as she got closer to climax and I kept at her, looking up at her face. I wanted to see her expression when I sent her over the edge.

I added a third finger and at the same time I thrust into her, I grazed my teeth over her clit. Her back arched up off the bed, her lips parted, and I knew I'd fucked up. I had to stop her from screaming out, from stretching her mouth wide and popping those stitches.

I threw myself forward and held her jaw up, forcing her mouth to stay shut. I pressed my cheek against hers.

"Shh, Tabitha. Shh, I'm sorry, *engill*. So fucking sorry. I didn't think."

Her body shook and I could feel her tears against my skin. I lifted up and looked down into her scared, confused expression.

"What happened?" she asked, voice trembling.

"You were about to cry out as you came and I realized you'd pop your stitches if you screamed so I rushed to stop you. I was worried grabbing your jaw like that would trigger you. Fuck, love, I'm sorry. That should have been a blissful experience. You should still be floating on your high and I fucked up."

She reached up and ran a finger down my nose before tapping my lips.

"It was amazing, Arrow. I've never felt like that before. And thank you for thinking about my stitches because I'd completely forgotten about them." She smirked as her gaze moved lower. "Your beard is a mess."

I laughed and reached up to run my palm over my beard, wiping away the remnants of her cream as best as I could.

"Totally worth it. You are the best thing I've ever tasted, and when those stitches come out, I'm gonna eat you out until you scream loud enough to rattle the fucking windows."

She ran her fingers through my hair and smiled up at me. Her eyes sparkled with joy and her cheeks were still flushed from her climax. She'd never looked more beautiful.

"Don't stop now. I promise I will keep my jaw locked shut the rest of the night."

With a heart lighter than it'd been in a very long time, I lowered down and pressed a kiss to the tip of her nose.

"Can't wait to be able to kiss your lips again."

Leaning over, I pulled out the drawer on my nightstand and grabbed a condom. I kneeled back between her legs and took in the sight she made as I rolled the latex over my cock.

"You sure about this? You wanna be mine? Because if you say yes to having sex with me, that's accepting my claim on you. You'll be mine. Only mine."

She fought to not grin. "I'll be your old lady?"

My breath caught as I smiled down at her. "Yeah, love, you'll be my old lady. You don't have a problem with that?"

She screwed up her nose. "You guys could have come up with something better than *old lady*, but I want to be yours, Arrow. When you're close, I feel complete."

With emotion stinging my eyes, I leaned forward over her and lined my cock up with her entrance. Locking my gaze with hers, I pressed forward, entering her for the first time.

"I love you, Tabitha."

Once I was fully buried within her, I lowered my face

down to hers and placed a light kiss to the center of her bottom lip, between the rows of stitches. Before I could lift back up, she pressed a palm to each of my cheeks, holding me still while she flicked her gaze between each of my eyes, as though she was searching for something. I didn't break the connection as I shifted my hips back, then back in, taking her slow and steady.

"Mine, *engill*. You're mine now."

The next glide in had her moaning and tilting her hips up to meet my stroke.

"I was always yours, Bodie Trygg. From the moment you took me in your arms, I've been yours."

After I rubbed the tip of my nose up the side of hers, I shifted back onto my knees. Running my palms up her thighs, I held her still as I set about fully claiming her.

Tabitha

Arrow was insatiable. He took me four times during the night and as the sun streaked through the window, I woke to his lips gliding over the back of my neck. He was spooned up behind me and he moved my leg back over his before running his fingers down my inner thigh until he found my slick entrance ready for him.

My lips parted on a moan. "Hmmm."

He pumped first two, then three fingers inside me, slowly building my arousal until I was squirming. His thick erection was between my ass cheeks and with every movement I made, he throbbed against me, making me want more.

"Need you inside me, Arrow," I whispered.

"No more gloves, love. I'll have to get you off with my hands this time."

I groaned. As talented as his fingers were, I wanted his dick inside me.

"I'm on the shot and I'm clean. Got tested after the rescue."

"You saying I can take you bare? Fill you up."

I chuckled at his possessive tone. Such a caveman. Or rather, Viking.

"If you're clean, yeah."

"Never had sex before without gloving up, and it's been a long damn time since I've done that."

Before I could ask about how long since he'd had sex, he shifted up and stole my breath when, gripping my hips, he brought me down over his dick.

I threw my head back, "Oh!"

He slid all the way in on the first glide and filled me completely. He snaked an arm around my front, palming my uninjured breast as he began to thrust in and out. With no condom between us, I could feel the ridge of his cock head as he pressed in and out of my channel. I was extra sensitive after him taking me so many times and it didn't take long before my arousal was spiraling high.

Releasing my breast, he rolled us over so I was facing the mattress, lifting my hips up so my butt was up in the air. He trailed his fingers down my spine.

"So fucking beautiful. And all mine."

He thrust back in, jolting my body with the force of each stroke he made. Panic began to creep in as my past tried to rise up and swallow me. He stilled as I pushed up on my arms and widened my knees so I could straighten up.

"Arrow…"

He thankfully heard the strain to my voice and pulled out of me before turning me around to face him, peppering kisses down the side of my face.

"I've got you, Tabitha. We're good. It's all good, my love."

He moved to lay back and he gripped my hips and set me over his pelvis. "You take the reins, *engill*."

Tears pricked my eyes at how sweet he was, at how much he got me and the ease with which he could pull me out of a spiral.

I reached down and gripped his slick dick with my hand, giving it a couple strokes before I rose up over the top of him. I rested a palm over his pec as I lowered myself down his length, not stopping until he was buried deep. With a moan, I began moving, alternating between swiveling my hips and shifting back and forth. Sweat slicked his skin and I marveled at how his cheeks flashed pink and his eyes dilated the closer he got.

"You go first, *engill*. You always go first."

He shifted his grip from my hip to tease my clit as I continued to move over him. I clenched my jaw against the scream that rose up my throat at the blast of pleasure that caused.

Two flicks later, I shattered, barely able to keep my mouth closed as my orgasm ripped through me, stealing my breath and sanity. As I floated on my high, his erection kicked inside me and a warm wash filled me. For a moment, I dreamed about what could be if I wasn't on birth control.

I collapsed down against his chest, and he wrapped his arms around me, enclosing me in the safety of his embrace. With a smile, I snuggled in.

Before I fell back asleep, I whispered the words I'd meant to say earlier before he distracted me with sex.

"Love you."

Epilogue

Arrow

Taz spent another two days interrogating Volt before he declared he was done. I didn't mind waiting; it gave me two more days to make love to Tabitha enough times that she was well and truly mine. Hopefully she wouldn't run after seeing me end Volt.

She kept assuring me she didn't have an issue with it. That she was fine with knowing I'd killed the men who raped Jacqueline. But knowing I'd done something and watching me do it, were two different things entirely and I was worried I'd lose her. Turned out I was like my father after all, and I was completely addicted to the woman I loved. I just prayed that, unlike my mother, Tabitha was equally addicted to me.

She sat next to me in one of the booths in the main bar area of the clubhouse and when I saw Scout coming our way, I tightened my hold on her while I leaned over to press a kiss to the top of her head.

"You ready?"

I nodded to Scout. "Yeah, let's get this done."

He turned to Tabitha. "You sure about this? You can't go back and un-see a man die."

She sat straighter and looked Scout in the eye. "I'm sure, Scout. I need to know he's gone. So he can't invade my dreams like Godfrey does."

Scout winced but nodded. There was nothing we could do about Godfrey. No way to bring him back so we could kill him again. No matter how much the fucker deserved it.

"Let's go then."

I took her hand in mine and prayed it wasn't for the last time, before I led her behind Scout, down the back staircase to the cells. Taz was down there waiting for us. He gave Tabitha a nod of respect as we filed into the room.

She slipped her palm from mine and moved over to where Volt hung, looking even worse than he had when I'd seen him two days ago. She went over to the table and ran her hand over the tools laying out before she wrapped her palm around the hilt of a knife. She moved back over to Volt and grabbed his jaw between her thumb and fingers and lifted his head so he was forced to look at her.

"Tabitha. My sweet Tabitha," he murmured.

I wanted to rip his tongue out for claiming her but Scout and Taz both stepped up and took hold of my arms.

"You gotta let her have this, brother. Let her have her closure. She's earned it."

Fuck. I knew Taz was right but dammit, I wanted to be the one to end this prick. To avenge my woman.

"I'm not now, nor have I ever been yours, Volt." She ran her gaze over him before she spoke again. "I was going to cut you up like Mia cut me, but now I find you're just not worth the effort. Or the mess."

She dropped her hand away from his face and turning, she tossed the knife back on the table before she came over to me. Smiling up at me, she blew me a kiss. "He's all yours, babe."

After pressing a kiss to her forehead and inhaling her scent, I moved her to where I'd been standing between Scout and Taz. Both men would catch her if she passed out, or follow her if she needed to leave the room.

"Prez, you want to say your bit?"

"Nah, you can do it. I've gotten to say it way too often lately."

I went over to the table where Taz had already laid out my pistol crossbow and bolts. Technically, they weren't an arrow, but they were close enough for me to claim the weapon. Still facing Tabitha, I lifted it up so she could see it clearly.

"There's another reason I'm called Arrow, love."

She smiled. "Well, naturally, that'd be your weapon of choice."

Fuck, she slayed me. She still showed no hint of panic or fear. She was so damn brave and strong.

Blowing out a breath, I turned to Volt, who was watching us.

"The Charon MC was named after the Greek Ferryman who, legend said, was the one who decided if a soul went to the Elysian Fields or Hades after death. You made a big fucking mistake creating Oblivion, and you fucked up even more by taking my woman. You've been judged and we're sending you straight to hell where you belong."

I held up my crossbow and aimed it at his heart. Ignoring the fact he was pissing himself, I hit the trigger. I didn't pull my gaze away until the light left his eyes. Then, I set the weapon back on the table before slowing turning to see Tabitha's reaction.

The tears streaming down her cheeks ripped me open until she lunged forward and plowed into me, wrapping her arms around my waist.

"He's really gone. I'm free. I'm really, truly free."

Tears stung my eyes as I wrapped her in my arms and held her tight. I still had her. She was still mine.

Thank fuck.

Tabitha

Packing the last of my clothes into a backpack, I closed it and slung it over my shoulder, grinning as I headed out of our room and downstairs to meet up with Arrow, who should be done with church by now. He was finally taking me for a ride on his bike. We were heading to his place down the coast for a few days of alone time.

I reached the front room just as the men filed out of their meeting room. Scout followed Arrow over to me.

"Before you lovebirds head off, I've got a few things I want to discuss with you," Scout said. "Head on back to my office. I'll be there in a sec."

He turned toward Blade as Arrow grabbed my hand and led me down a hallway.

"We're not in trouble, are we? He's not going to stop us from going?"

"Not sure what he wants to talk to us about, but we're not in trouble. At least, not that I know of."

He winked at me and I relaxed a little, but I still didn't like not knowing what was going on. We'd been waiting in his office for about ten minutes when Scout finally came through the door, along with a few others. Todd, Blade, Cindy, Keys, Donna, and Mirabelle all filed in, making the office rather crowded.

"Right. I haven't taken this to the club to vote on yet because I want your take on it first. If you're not all on board, there's no point in going any further. Jacqueline is onboard already."

Jacqueline couldn't remember anything of her rape thanks to the fact she'd been given Oblivion, but she knew what had happened to her and had the physical bruises to show her the truth. I'd spoken to her for the first time yesterday and her abuse had strengthened her resolve to help others.

"I want us to set up a crisis center here in Bridgewater. Not just an office for Jacqueline, but a full-on center that will cater to all the needs of sexual abuse and human trafficking survivors. As a club, we're going to keep going after Godfrey's associates and victims. We're going to keep finding more women—and men—who need a safe place to heal and get better. I'm inviting you all to be involved with it from the start. What do you say?"

I swiped the tears from my face and pushed through the others until I could give Scout a hug.

"Thank you. I'm in. Whatever I can do."

The others all followed suit with their agreement to be a part of it.

Todd cleared his throat. "Does this mean I can't keep working at the shop?"

Scout chuckled. "No, son, you're always welcome to keep coming to the shop."

"Great. Then I'm in, too."

I moved from Scout back to Arrow, running my palm over Todd's arm on my way past. Physical touch was still difficult for him to handle but I wanted him to know I loved him.

Scout dismissed us and we all filed out to the main room where there was more space for everyone.

Still stunned, I slipped my hand into Arrow's. "I can't believe Scout's doing this."

Arrow hugged me close, kissing my temple. "He ain't doing it alone. We're all going to do it. It's a great idea. And we're going to be able to really help anyone we find in the future."

An idea came to me and I gasped. "I know what we should call it!"

Arrow shook his head, grinning. "If it's not Greek, don't even think about it."

I frowned. "Greek?"

"Yeah. You haven't noticed all the club businesses are named after Greek gods or rivers or some other fucked-up ancient Greek thing?"

I shook my head. "That's crazy. What about Retro Funk and Marie's Cafe? Or Silky Ink?"

"They're not technically owned by the club, *engill*."

"That just stupid. Where's Scout?"

I went looking for him and found him talking to Blade and Veronica about the planned center.

"Scout? Can I suggest a name?" I asked.

He shrugged. "Sure, but the club has to vote on it."

"Pieces to Peace."

Veronica gasped, her eyes filling with tears. "Oh, that's beautiful. Please, Scout, let us use that for the name."

Scout rolled his eyes. "Brothers, control your women. I said the club had to vote on it."

Arrow wrapped his arm around my waist and pulled me back against his warmth.

"You know we're all gonna vote that shit through without a problem," he said.

Grinning, surrounded by friends and family, I wanted to burst with the joy that rose up within me. My life had meaning. I had a plan that would fill my days with something meaningful and a good man who would have my back through it all.

For the first time in forever, I couldn't wait for the future.

Other Charon MC Books:

Book 1:
Inking Eagle

Eagle & Silk

Book 2:
Fighting Mac

Mac & Zara

Book 3:
Chasing Taz

Taz & Zara

240

Book 4:

Claiming Tiny

Tiny & Mercedes (Missy)

Book 5:

Saving Scout

Scout & Marie

Book 6:

Tripping Nitro

Nitro & Cindy

Book 7:

Scout's Legacy

Scout & Marie

Book 8:

Mac's Destiny

Mac & Zara

Book 9:

Losing Bash

Bash

Book 10:

Finding Needles

Needles & Bess

Book 11:

Forging Blade

Blade & Veronica

Book 12:

Taming Keys

Keys & Donna

243

www.ingramcontent.com/pod-product-compliance
Lightning Source LLC
Chambersburg PA
CBHW070555120726
47909CB00007B/2355